CRUEL STAKES

VAMPIRES & VICES NO. 2

NINA WALKER

ADDISON & GRAY PRESS

Cover Design by Yocla Book Cover Designs

Paperback ISBN: 978-1-950093-27-4

Ebook ISBN: 978-1-950093-23-6

Addison & Gray Press, LLC

To the ones who saved me

CHAPTER 1 - ADRIAN

I swirl the wine glass until the blood licks the edges. Then I drink, trying to ignore the taste and force my mind somewhere else. As always, it's impossible. The blood fills my mouth with delicious sensations, and I automatically savor every drop. My fangs burst forward as I swallow, aching for more. My mind goes blissfully numb.

My thoughts travel back to my childhood until I lock on a safe memory––one of the many times I devoured a pomegranate. Every autumn they would come back in season, and I would break them open to gorge on the seeds like they were candy. I cling to that thought as I drink from the wine glass, eyes closed, imagining the blood is the same as that tangy-sweet fruit I once loved so much. The plump crimson seeds would burst, and the juice would run down my cheeks and neck, often staining my tunic or my chest.

In most of my early childhood memories us boys only wore clothing when it was cold. Nakedness was normal for the Hellenes––the Greeks. Another reminder that so much has changed since those far off days of youth. Nakedness has come and gone out of style over the centuries, same as nearly everything else. With every resurgence fads will slightly change, molded to fit the current generations' tastes, until they eventually no longer resemble the original.

But the pomegranates still grow in Greece.

The buildings corroded, the treasures were stolen by new empires, the culture changed, the language evolved, and even my devout mother's religion became nothing but myths for twisting into cautionary tales––but the pomegranates stayed.

I finish off the glass and set it down, watching the last beads of blood slide into a little pool at the bottom. I eye it, reminded of a time when I'd have licked the glass clean. There was also a time when I'd have thrown the full glass and shattered it in a fit of rage, going hungry as the blood grew cold. That is, when I drank from a glass at all. Things also used to be entirely different between the vampires and humans. We used to take their lives freely, killing with almost every meal. We're much more civilized these days . . . well, mostly more civilized.

For now, I find myself settled somewhere between self-loathing of who I've become and bitter acceptance of everything I've lost.

Blood will always be my tormentor as it is my liberator.

I will always crave it and need it, like an addict bargaining for his next fix. It will always bind me to an afterlife I did not choose and to a woman I hate. Most vampires love their makers, but how could I love Brisa when she took away my agency and made me immortally thirsty against my will? She may claim to love me, I may be one of her eldest sons, but I'm still a single root in her tree, a lone bee in her nest, and a thin thread in her rope.

I close my eyes for another moment, gathering my thoughts as the fog clears, then open my computer and pull up the video conferencing software. It's a good thing Brisa's paranoid and refuses to leave France, because if she were here to question me about Hugo's death, she'd probably sense the truth.

And the last thing the vampire queen needs to know is the truth.

The screen brightens and there she is, the creature who followed me home from The Lyceum after another day of studying at the feet of master philosophers all those lifetimes ago. She'd sunk her teeth into me and stolen my mortality as well as a bright future among my peers. I'd been in agony, begging for my life, when she'd buried me and left me to my own devices three nights later. I crawled from the grave in a wave of bloodthirst and made my way back home. I was lucky the sunrise didn't get me. Or maybe not, because the deaths that followed have haunted me for centuries.

I had killed my own family––ripping the lives from my wife and our unborn child. And I've never forgiven myself or Brisa since.

Pushing those thoughts aside, I smile warmly at her now. "Hello, Mother. You look stunning."

And she does, she always does. So that's not a lie. But I will lie to her today, as I learned how to do quickly under her tutelage. I'm still not able to refuse her commands outright. However, lying is a skill I've developed as one would slowly introduce poison to their bloodstream in order to become immune. It was painful, slow and terrible, but it was well worth it. Now there's little she can do to control me unless it's an outright command.

"Do you find it strange that you call me mother considering we've been lovers?" she asks, batting her eyelashes.

My stomach hardens. I was her lover, at first, because I was lost to the bloodlust as many new vampires are. She came to me in my weakest moment and offered me answers and a warm bed. When the years passed and I was able to rise above the bloody haze of youth, my hatred for her grew like an infection, and then I was only her lover because I didn't want her to question my loyalty. She would've killed me if she thought I was a threat. I've seen her do it countless times. And I didn't want to die until I could enact my revenge for what she did to me.

Even to this day, if she calls me to her bed, I will go. And I will hate her even more.

"I will stop calling you mother if you wish." I laugh, playing her game, and actually I would like nothing better. She commanded me to call her mother when she first found me, and I've had no choice but to comply ever since. My real mother was nothing like Brisa. She was kind and warm and spirited. And even though her bones are dust, I often think of her and what could have been.

And then I think of all those I killed, and force my mind blank.

"Hmm," Brisa muses, "let's keep "mother" for now. And speaking of, when are you going to visit me?" She smirks at the screen and raises an eyebrow. "I do miss you, darling."

I've been in New Orleans for a handful of decades, and while part of me misses traveling, I've already seen all there is to see on this earth while being limited to darkness. As for now, I rather enjoy running the businesses. It gives me something purposeful to do. And as much as some humans hate it––Evangeline comes to mind––our setup protects the humans. If we didn't have willing donors, we would be forced to go back to murdering for our food. We'd be relegated back to the shadows, hiding among the fringes of society, and most vampires would never stand for that. We've gotten a taste of this new way of living and we like the control. Take it away and there would be war, chaos, and endless bloodshed.

And we absolutely can't bite a human and leave them alive with our venom running through their veins. It makes them far too dangerous to our kind, ruthless hunters who can track our movements and fight us with nearly equal strength. Again, Eva comes to mind.

"Adrian!" Brisa cuts off my thoughts. She turns to face the camera head-on and glares. "Are you paying attention, or are you wasting my time?"

"My apologies." I'm quick to recover. "As soon as you order me back to France, of course I will come, but for now I am rather busy here. I think you'd like modern day New Orleans. Are you sure you can't come visit me instead?"

I know she'll refuse, but I'd love to get her into a position of vulnerability. She is the queen because she is the head of the remaining vampiric bloodlines. She's worked hard to ensure there are no vampires left to challenge her, and her own maker is long dead. She's placed strong and loyal princes around her--always sons--but none of us would be able to assume the position of king unless the entire family was gone, save for one.

That will never happen.

And there are no princesses to angle for queen. Brisa has never confessed why she doesn't turn women, but I know it's because she doesn't want anyone to rival her beauty and power. That, and she doesn't sleep with women, so she can't use them up the way she does her princes.

"You know I can't travel anymore," she sighs dramatically. "I did this to myself."

And that's true.

"But at least my new home is beautiful." She shifts the camera to reveal a room gilded in gold, and my mouth falls open——something that hasn't happened in ages. I've been around so long that I can't remember the last time I was surprised, but this is truly unexpected. "Isn't it amazing?" she coos. "The French people were finally generous enough to hand over my favorite city." Her eyes gleam, and she leans forward, her voice lowering. "It belongs to us now."

City.

I recognize exactly where she is——the famous city of Versailles. The very same one that King Louis XIV built and was named the capital of the country for years. I always believed in my maker's ability to get her way but even I'll admit I didn't think she'd manage this one.

But she did.

She's set up in the palace and, if she's taken over the city, then that means she has achieved a lifelong goal of hers: to compel enough of the governmental officials in France, forcing them to turn over France's prized jewel. This is something she's been trying to accomplish since well before we first came out of hiding, but the French people have been better at eluding us compared to many of the others.

"*You* are amazing," I respond coolly. "Honestly, Mother, I am in awe of you."

Her weakness is her own vanity.

"Yes, yes." Her face relaxes. "Now, what was it you wished to speak to me about?"

This is it. Although she may already know. Makers can sense these things through the blood bonds, but with an ocean between them, it's a bit diluted.

"Hugo is dead."

Her face stills, turning to stone. "How did it happen?" she finally asks. Her voice is eerily quiet, a sign of the rage behind her calm exterior.

So she didn't know. That's interesting—and promising. Now it's time to tell her the story I've created to protect Eva. The human girl killed Hugo exactly as I had orchestrated, and I'd feel bad about how I manipulated her if she hadn't come asking for trouble.

"You told him that if he caught my fledgling in a lie, then he could have her for himself," I say, narrowing my eyes.

She laughs. "That's right. I almost forgot about that." I dig my fingers into my chair to keep from outright glaring because I highly doubt that's true. The woman never forgets anything. "And he succeeded?" Her eyes thin into knowing slits. "Did you bring a hunter into your own home?"

"The girl was foolish and was trying to get in with

both groups. The hunters ambushed us in the cemetery and killed Hugo. They almost got me too." My voice grows angry, "I will avenge my brother, of this I swear."

She doesn't say anything for a moment, and the tiny flame of worry ignites in my chest. If she can sense the inferno, then I'm already dead. "And what of the girl? Please tell me she's dead too."

"She's not." I shrug as if I couldn't care less about Eva either way. "She wishes to be freed and to live out her life as a human." I smirk. "I think we scared her away, Mother." I don't say anything more. Sometimes it's imperative to know when to stop and this is one of those moments.

Brisa considers this, and for a moment I'm certain she's going to order me to kill Eva. I'd have no choice. "Keep her as your prodigy," she says at last. "We need to watch her closely, but I have a feeling she may be of more use to us. Anyone who has the guts to play both sides is someone I want to entertain."

"You do enjoy playing games with human lives."

"Always." She winks.

Keeping Eva close is the opposite of what I had planned, but at least I don't have to kill her yet. I nod readily, my anxiety uncoiling like a spring.

"Are you absolutely sure those were hunters who killed Hugo?" she questions.

"Of course." The lie sounds a little shaky, and I grind my foot into the floor. I'm losing my touch, I can't let that happen, especially not over a ridiculous human. "Could they have been something else?"

We both know what that something else is I'm referring to. Brisa never likes to talk about them, she says it gives them power. I find that a foolish approach.

"I don't know." Her lips thin. "But Hugo isn't the only prince to have been murdered in the last few weeks."

This is news.

This is news that could change *everything*.

Brisa knows it. I know it. And we don't have to say anything more about it. If I were to question her further, she might suspect me. There are normally seven princes––one for each continent––but Brisa had eight when she sent Hugo and I to North America. He should've stayed in Mexico City as we planned, but a few years ago he decided he wanted to be in New Orleans just to spite me. So if he's gone, and at least one other too, then there can't be more than six of us left. I'd kill to know who else is gone, but I want to live so I don't ask.

"Watch your back, Adrianos," she offers before ending the call abruptly.

I close the computer, my mind whirling with possibility. "You'd better watch your back as well, *Mother*," I whisper to the dark. Then I pick up the phone and instruct Kelly to set up a meeting with Evangeline.

CHAPTER 2

One thing I've learned in my nineteen years—— vampires are excellent lie detectors. Their heightened senses allow them to smell when adrenaline enters the bloodstream. They can hear when a heart beats faster, and even detect the slightest change in a human's voice or mannerisms. Lying to one is about the most ridiculous thing a human can do, which is all I can think about as I ride the elevator up to Adrian's office prepared to lie my butt off. I've got to be either the bravest or the dumbest person I know. And I'm leaning toward the latter, but hey, nobody's perfect.

I was done with him——I never had to come back here ever again.

And that's the truth. Adrian and I had parted ways. I'd gotten what I wanted, my mother was free of her addictions, and Adrian had no hold over me anymore. I'd figured out that the blood vow was a complete lie, so there was no obligation for me to hold up my end of the deal, and Adrian wasn't going to make me. Hugo was dead, which was enough to make him happy and forget all about me. Plus, he was going to cover for me with Queen Brisa. It was all tidied away, and that was supposed to be the end of it.

So then why am I surrounded by the familiar reflective gold mirrors of his elevator, heading up to meet with him again? Because like I said, I'm an idiot. A brave idiot, but still an idiot. I never should've let Seth convince me to do this, but he knows as well as I that I want to help the hunters––even to my own detriment. I'm pretty sure I am about to regret that entire ideology pretty soon.

I gaze up at the ceiling, and a slightly distorted version of my face reflects back at me. I'm wearing a simple, red tank top and black pants with a wooden stake strapped under my pant leg just above the ankle. Adrian is probably going to freak if he notices it, and he will notice. He always does. Or maybe he doesn't actually sense the stakes I wear, maybe the man can read me like a book and knows I'm unlikely to go anywhere without one.

I groan and lean back into the corner, biting my bottom lip. I really shouldn't keep taking these chances. Adrian is a ruthless killer, a vampire prince with centuries of experience in staying alive and killing others to do it. No way am I going to keep getting away with lying to someone like that. He'll know better. He'll figure out that I am here as a double agent and he'll kill me without hesitation. Sure, I can fight--I've been working hard in training and this venom from Hugo has enhanced my senses--but I'm still outmatched by Mr. Adrianos "Runs the City" Teresi, aka Adrian.

I reach out toward the red button, ready to turn this elevator around and never look back.

Too late--the elevator dings, and the doors slide open as if to mock me.

I slow my breathing, square my shoulders, and step into Adrian's office.

Nothing has changed. It's still polished oak and professional and not welcoming for someone like me. I shouldn't have come the first time, and I shouldn't be here now. This is a lion's den. Actually, Adrian is less of a lion and more of a snake considering what he does with his mouth. *Don't think about what he does with his mouth.*

I inhale--nice and slow--willing my heart to slow the heck down. He can't know I'm here to lie. *He can't know, he can't know, he can't know*--unless he already does.

"It's my birthday today," I say, making sure my voice has the snarky quality I reserve specially for him. "Last night I went to bed as a salty eighteen-year-old, and today I woke up a salty nineteen."

And that's true. Maybe if I sprinkle in truth with the lies he'll believe every word.

But probably not.

The man is sitting at his desk, his face unreadable and his eyes glued to his computer. He doesn't acknowledge me. The elevator doors close. I stand there, afraid to move.

Finally, he looks up, those glacial eyes locking with mine, and does the last thing I expect. He smiles. It's such a rarity, I'm momentarily stunned. He's already beautiful considering the vampire DNA enhanced those attractive Greek features, so it's not my fault that I'm staring because humans are hardwired to be attracted to vampires. Not. My. Fault. He's still a sucker and a murderer, and I'll continue to hate him . . . even if he did save my mother.

"Well, you never claimed to be sweet," he says at last.

For a moment I forget what I said about being salty, but it comes back to me, and my cheeks warm. "True." I shake myself from whatever trance I'm under and sit down in the chair across from him. "You know, it amazes me that in this messed up vampire world there are still people who celebrate their birth. Do you know some humans celebrate their entire birthday month like it's some kind of holiday? I can't even stomach thinking about growing older for a single day, let alone for all of September."

He leans back and steeples his fingers together. "This world has been messy long before vampires came out to play. Are you sure this"––he pauses for a moment, considering–– "tantrum isn't because of your personality?"

I'm not sure if he's joking using that word "tantrum" but maybe I am being childish. Is he joking? I'm not even angry about it, though, and against my better judgement, I laugh. "True that. Those astrology-obsessed people out there would say my saltiness is typical for a virgo."

"Do you know how much astrology has changed over the years, Angel? You shouldn't put too much stock into something as pliable as astrology."

Don't let Ayla hear you say that. My bestie loves that stuff. To her, the stars are forever and they make the rules.

"Trust me, I'm not. I already know I'm feeling extra salty today because I'm one year closer to my prefrontal cortex developing and my brain becoming vampire playdough."

He laughs, and something loosens in my chest. This is weird. This banter feels like a normal interaction between friends, or maybe even flirting. Part of me wants to soften into it, but the smarter part of me listens to the inner-alarm bells: danger, danger, danger.

Adrian is not *Adrian.*

Adrian is *Adrianos Teresi*––vampire prince and ruthless killer. End of story.

"Do you know what amazes me? That you're still coming into my casino with stakes strapped to your ankle." He stands in one fluid movement.

"Are you going to take it from me?" I don't move. Besides, I expected this.

He circles, coming up behind me, and whispers low in my ear. "No, you keep it." And then he straightens and is back into his chair before I can blink. I'm not sure what to do with this information, but him letting me keep it is unsettling. He's never done that before.

Actually, that's not true. He was happy to let me keep it when he wanted me to kill Hugo for him. I'm still mad about being used like that, but I guess we're even considering what he did for my mother.

"So what did you want to talk to me about?" I ask. When I called yesterday to set up this meeting, Kelly had said Adrian wanted to speak with me as well. I'd be lying if I said that hadn't piqued my interest.

"Better question is what did you want to talk to me about?" He's staring. I don't know what to do with a staring Adrian. I wasn't planning on this kind of attention from a man who's always been so aloof with me.

But I know what I have to do, even if I'm terrified to do it. "Nope, I asked you first."

He opens his drawer and pulls out a black box. "I got you a birthday present."

Of all things he could've done right now, this one surprises me the most. My mouth pops open. What the heck? He knew it was my birthday? He's giving me a present? What alternate timeline did I step into, because I'm pretty sure this can't be my life?

"I don't know what to say except what have you done with the real Adrianos Teresi? Are you his long lost twin or something?"

He tosses the box at me with an annoyed sigh. "Just open it."

"Well, there's the vampire I know and hate."

"At your service." He chuckles under his breath and my stomach tightens.

The gift is in what looks like a jewelry box, so that's what I'm expecting when I open it. Nope. Not jewelry. "Are you kidding me right now?" I pull out a set of car keys and turn them over in my hands. They're heavy, and when I read the Porsche label, I drop them on the desk with a metallic clatter. "No, no freaking way. I can't accept this."

He has the audacity to look offended. "You can and you will. It's waiting for you in the garage. You need a car, don't you? I figured this would be a suitable gift."

"Okay, first of all, you getting me a gift at all is beyond weird, but second of all, this is way too extravagant. People are going to ask where I got it."

Not to mention, a gift from a vampire has to be a trick, especially one this nice.

"Are you worried about your hunters? Tell them you won it." His eyes are unreadable. "That's not so unbelievable."

"Uh, yes it is. People don't really win cars, Adrian. They give away their email addresses hoping to win cars and then spend an eternity unsubscribing from the same scammy dealerships." I can't believe I'm doing this, but I plop the keys back in the box and slide them across the desk. "I'm serious. Forget the fact that a Porsche is way too nice for a girl like me; I'd never be able to make up a story that people would believe."

His eyes darken. "It is *not* too nice for you, so I don't ever want to hear you say that again."

I snort. I don't know how to take that.

Adrian eyes the box for a moment. "Fine. How about I play you for it? We are in a casino after all." He opens his desk drawer again and produces a set of shiny dice. They look like silver, but they can't be since vampires are allergic to it. The metal doesn't kill them, but it weakens them. There's no silver in this entire place, save for the little crucifix under my shirt. The dice must be made from a different kind of metal since he's handling them easily. They shine under the warm lights with undertones of gold.

"We'll play it craps style. You roll the dice," he says, "if it's a seven or eleven, you win, if it's a two, three, or twelve, then I win. And if it's something else, you keep rolling."

"I already know you have telekinesis, so nice try, but no."

He reaches out and cups my hand in his cold ones. A pulse of electricity shoots up my spine, and my senses grow to double. For a moment, my mind goes so sharp it almost hurts, but Adrian doesn't seem to notice a thing. "I promise I won't cheat," he whispers. When he releases my hand, the dice are resting in my palm.

"But you have the advantage," I protest, already

finding myself giving in to him. "You have three numbers to win on, and I only have two."

"Ah, but statistically, seven is the most common number rolled between two dice." He winks. "And besides, you know the house has to keep some advantage. That's the way gambling works, but it doesn't mean you can't win."

Well, the fact that vampires are running this place is already advantageous enough, but I don't say that. He's not going to let this go, and as much as I hate to admit this, I'm intrigued. And part of me, surely the foolish part, the part that grew up poor, the part that never had anything nice for herself, the part that desperately wants to feel loved and worthy and maybe even wealthy-- really wants that car.

"Okay," I whisper, and then I roll the dice.

CHAPTER 3

a three and a five. Nobody wins.

"Again," he says.

I repeat the process and we get another roll where nobody wins, but this time it's a six. I've been dancing around a winning roll, and despite my better judgement, I'm ready to beat him. *No.* No, I'm not. I'm not ready to beat him. I know what I want but I also know what I should want, and they're two very different things. I close my eyes for a second, unable to untangle my thoughts, then shake them away and blow on the dice for good luck.

I roll.

They clink across the desk, landing on two ones--snake eyes. Adrian wins.

Or maybe we both do . . .

He hands me the black box and says, "I don't want to hear another word about it."

I want the car--I don't want the car--I'm mixed up and wouldn't even know what to say about it. Everything is brighter, somehow. Impossibly bright, like the sun is blasting through those tinted windows. I blink rapidly. Maybe I should leave.

"Now, what was it that you wanted to talk to me about?" he questions.

This is the fun part. Not.

"I want to be your fledgling." I swallow hard. "For real this time."

He freezes, a bewildered expression crossing his face, and I think maybe I'm the one to surprise him this time. His eyes narrow into two blue orbs--again, snake eyes. "You're a vampire hunter. Don't forget that I know what you are. Why would I trust you with this request?"

I sit up taller. "Because Cameron was right."

"Cameron?" He says it like the name means little to him.

"Yes, Cameron. You know, Kelly's prodigy, the one who is also a hunter?"

"Of course I know who he is, but what does he have to do with you?" His tone goes sour.

Maybe he doesn't like Cameron, which is interesting considering he's in line to join the family tree. I tuck that information away for later. "He showed me something that changed everything." I boldly recite the words I'd rehearsed at home about fifty times this morning. "I know there are some kind of energy demons out there who are your enemies, and that's why you wanted me to get information about Leslie Tate. He's one of them. I thought I was working for the good guys when I joined the hunters, but I realize now that's not true. Cameron was right. If I don't join you, then eventually I'll end up dead. I'd rather have immortality than become some demon's meal."

Lies. Lies. Lies.

And in all honesty, learning about these demonish energy stealers only made me want to protect humans even more, but Adrian doesn't have to know that. He stands again and saunters over to peer out his window. Since windows at the Alabaster Heart are heavily tinted and bulletproof, he can see the sun without being burned by it. I wonder how many years he lived in the dark and what that must have been like for him. I couldn't do it, myself. The sun means too much to me. I watch him as he looks down on the Mississippi river and let myself drink him in. He's tall and handsome and tortured. And in his suit, he almost looks human.

Not for the first time, I wish he was.

"Come here, please," he says softly.

I don't know if I've ever heard that word from his mouth, but if he's going to believe that I want him to one day become my maker, then I'd better lose the attitude and start doing what he asks. Damn, I should've thought this one through more. Attitude is sort of my calling card. And now I have to suck up to a blood sucker? I can't think of anything worse.

But I go stand at his side.

Between the blinking of my eyes, he's beside me one second and in front of me the next. My back presses to the warm window as his cold hand grips my throat. It's not so tight that he's strangling me, but it's a promise of what's to come if I don't get the next few moments right.

"You're a terrible liar," he says, his voice low and dangerous. "The last thing you want to become is like me." He's so close now, glaring down at me, his fangs extending.

"That's not true," I hiss. But I know he's already won.

"Really?" He nods toward my leg. "Then why are you still carrying a stake with you?"

My mind races for an answer. "Because this building houses a vampire coven, and I'm not a complete idiot."

"That's debatable." He shakes his head. "You're here to double cross me."

I don't know what to do. He's figured me out in about point-two seconds flat, and now he's going to kill me. My heart pounds, and my hands clench and unclench. I want to run, but there's nowhere to go. His hand tightens, and my breath goes shallow. I automatically reach up and grab onto his wrists, trying to get free. It does nothing.

"You saved my mother," I whisper-hiss. "You were the only one who would've done that for me. And after everything, I think maybe vampires aren't so bad after all."

"Vampires aren't bad after all?" He laughs but doesn't

release me. My air supply is dwindling fast. "Like I said, you're a terrible liar."

"Why don't we roll the dice? If I win, you let me stay as your prodigy, and if you win, I'll leave you alone," I squeak out in little bursts.

He frees me, and my knees weaken. I lean back against the window for support and gulp in big breaths of the overly conditioned air. He's lightning fast, returning for the dice and dropping them at my feet. "You keep those. Take them with your car."

"You don't want to roll dice?"

"I am tired of games," he snaps. "You need to leave now."

I jut my hip and raise an eyebrow. "What about being your prodigy?"

He slinks into his desk chair. "Fine, Angel. I'll take you up on whatever this foolish venture of yours is, but don't think I believe this will end well for you."

"So--"

"You can be my fledgling."

"Thank you." I shoot him a winning smile, but it doesn't faze him one bit.

"Don't thank me, yet. I haven't turned you into my prodigy, and I doubt I ever will." His fangs have receded into his gums when he smiles grimly back at me. I have no idea what he's thinking, and I'd give my right leg to be able to crawl into that brain of his and know every last thought. "But we will continue this charade and see where it leads us."

"I won't let you down," I say cheerily, like a girl scout who made her biggest sale. Quite frankly, it's no wonder he's already called me out. We both know this is a farce, right? And if that's the case, his agreement should scare the snot out of me. "So, you'll let me know what I'm supposed to do next, right? Like, is there some kind of initiation or a test or something?" This right here is information I'm dying to take back to my hunter team. He probably knows that.

"Kelly will get in touch soon. And, Angel, this means you're still spying on Tate for me."

"When he gets back." I nod, because what else can I say at this point?

"Yes. And he will be back, I'm sure of it. The man wants to see me dead and he can't very well do that without his hunters, now can he? In the meantime, I need you to do something else for me as well."

My heartbeat speeds up, which I'm certain he can hear. "Anything," I say brightly. Okay, I'm totally a *lying* girl scout because I'm not willing to do anything. In fact, I'm willing to do very little for vampires, even sexy ones with arctic eyes and golden wavy hair. Even ones who saved my own mother.

"Lose your virginity."

He speaks of my virginity like it's an item on a checklist.

"Excuse me?" My cheeks prickle, and my senses jump up again. I'm keenly aware of everything in this room, my own embarrassment most of all.

He holds my gaze and tilts his head slightly. "You heard me, Angel. I can't have you around my coven with your blood smelling like that, it's too . . . distracting."

"Uhhh--" My face reddens. "Sorry, but I'm not going to lose my virginity until I'm ready."

He tries to look surprised, but mostly he just looks smug. "Oh, but you said you'd do anything."

"Yeah, but--"

"Then make yourself ready and take care of it." He sweeps his hand toward me in a leave-me-alone-you-peon motion. I glare at him, but I do what he says and get into the elevator. What else can I do? The doors close, and I find myself looking up again at my reflection.

Absolutely nothing about this meeting went as planned, but at least I made it out alive.

CHAPTER 4

Kelly meets me in the hotel lobby, and considering her puckered lips and sour gaze, I realize I'm not out of the woods quite yet.

"You know, you'd be gorgeous if you didn't glare all the time," I say, half-snarky and half-honest. She's absolutely stunning, smiling or not, but everytime I'm around her she's as angry as a cat in water––and that anger is usually directed toward me.

"Who says I care about being pretty?" she barks at me. Okay, maybe she's an angry dog––a possessive one, pissed that her master has allowed me to infiltrate her territory. "Or that a smile is a prerequisite."

"Sorry, that was rude of me to say." I give her an apologetic smile. "And actually, I like where you're going with that. Makes sense to me. Honestly, Kelly, I think you're a woman after my own heart. We could be friends."

"Ew." She rolls her eyes. "Come on then, let's go get your birthday present."

I follow her through the casino to the parking garage, my mind whirling with everything I've gotten myself into. Is the dice game simply that—a game? Did Adrian call Kelly while I was taking the elevator down from his office? Part of me is disappointed that Adrian isn't showing me the car himself, but that's a ridiculous thing to be disappointed about.

The vampire's parking garage isn't the same one that's open to the public for the hotel and casino guests. First of all, it's the nicest parking garage I've ever seen. The walls are painted a gleaming white and the ceilings and floor are matte black tile. There's gray carpet along the edges, and it even smells clean and welcoming. The lighting is terribly dim, but my eyes adjust far quicker than they used to—a side effect of Hugo's venom. As I take in the rows and rows and *rows* of collectable cars, I try not to salivate. They're in all colors and sizes, from SUVs to race cars to muscle cars and everything in between. Even a whole bunch of pretty motorcycles are mixed in and I wonder what it would be like to drive one. I've never even ridden on one before, but I'd love the chance.

"This way," Kelly nods toward the back of the garage, "and stay close to me. We don't need a repeat of what happened in the lobby."

She's referring to one of Hugo's baby prodigies

smelling the wound inflicted on me by the mob. The vamp had tried to eat me.

"I don't plan on ever coming here with an open wound again," I say.

And it's not like people don't bleed in the casino all the time. They do. But apparently my virgin blood mixed with the tiniest amount of that vampire venom from my first kill had made me irresistible to Hugo's bloodline. Now that he's dead, they're beholden to Brisa, and I wonder what she'd do if she found out about me.

I can only imagine that bloodlust has grown considering how long Hugo had his fangs in me that night he tried to turn me. The memory slices like a knife and I shiver. I hate to think of how close I came to becoming one of these monsters. And now, here I am, signing up to be Adrian's fledgling. What was I thinking? I'm still not sure how I'm going to get out of it in the end, but I have to lock that thought away or else I'm going to lose my nerve.

Kelly looks at me sidelong. "Honey, if I were a bee, then you would be the sweetest flower in the middle of spring." She says it like it's the most annoying thing on earth.

"Ah, thank you," I bat my eyelashes, "nobody's ever called me a flower before."

"Don't flatter yourself," she grumbles, "let me think of a better analogy."

"Don't worry." I touch her arm. "I liked that one."

Her skin is ice cold, reminding me of when Adrian

took my hand, and also reminding me that I could be exactly like them soon if I'm not careful. She brushes me off, ending the conversation. Maybe she can't think of a better analogy, or maybe she's warming up to me.

I laugh to myself because the thought of a sucker getting warm is ludicrous.

"What's so funny?"

"Nothing."

"I swear, I'm going to kill Adrian," she grumbles, but I know she doesn't mean it. Her love of her master is evident. I don't detect jealousy from her, only annoyance that she has to keep dealing with me. Hey, maybe even for an eternity.

We approach a line of cars at the back of the garage, and I can't help but gawk. They're definitely the nicest ones down here. I can't say for sure how I know that they're the best of the lot, but I can just tell by looking at them––they scream money.

Old money.

Big money.

Blood money.

"I guess congratulations are in order," she sighs. "Honestly, I don't know how you pulled this off, but I have to hand it to you. You've got Adrian wrapped around your finger."

"Uhhh, what?" I frown at her. "I didn't do anything, and I certainly never asked for a car. I refused it, if you must know, but he––"

"That's for you," she cuts me off and points to a

gorgeous black sports car. I blink in surprise. I don't know what I was expecting, especially considering everything else down here, but it certainly wasn't this. The car is beyond beautiful and has to be wildly expensive. It's little and curvy and sexy as hell. I've never thought of cars as sexy before but I've been corrected in my ways. I stare at it, suddenly caring very much about this piece of machinery. "You did something. Let's see . . . Hugo's dead, and the story is that hunters killed him." Kelly looks at me sidelong. "Which is quite interesting considering your background."

"I can't--"

She holds up her hand. "Don't say anything. It's better that I don't know the details." She runs the tips of her fingers across the shiny finish of the car. "This is a brand new Porsche 911 Carrera 4." She may as well be speaking Russian. "Which is completely lost on you, isn't it?"

I nod, but this time I grin. "I know less about cars than I know about astrophysics."

"What do you know about astrophysics?"

"Absolutely nothing."

Her lips quirk. I don't know why, but I want her to like me, and I'd love to make her laugh. It doesn't really make sense since she's the enemy, but I can't help but tease her. "Well, don't get too excited. This is not even close to being the nicest car Adrian owns," she continues, nodding toward the other cars in the row, "but it's still way too nice for someone who doesn't appreciate cars."

I'm starting to enjoy our banter far too much. "Oh, honey, I can appreciate this one." I wink. I click the unlock button on the key fob, open the driver's door, and climb inside. The maroon interior leather smells new and expensive. It kind of reminds me of the inside of a wallet.

"He didn't really give this to you." Kelly leans in through the open door, her ghostly face inches from mine. Her movements are fast and fluid and vampiric in a way I'll never get used to. "Adrian's name is on the title, and it's insured under his policy, so don't think you can go sell it." As if I would! Okay, maybe I would if I really needed to because this is way too expensive and completely unnecessary. Before I can utter a response, she slams the door in my face and dashes off.

"Well, that went well," I mutter to the steering wheel.

I wait there for a while, trying to figure out my next step. Should I go back upstairs and refuse to take something so fancy and ask for something more normal? Should I demand Adrian put the car in my name since it's a gift and I don't want him to lord it over me later? But no, I can't bring myself to do either, because every second I sit down here alone is another second a vampire could sniff me out and decide I'd make a great lunch.

I'll have to deal with whatever strings come attached to this beauty later.

I turn it on, and the engine is so quiet and smooth that I almost don't believe I'm doing this right. I carefully drive from the dark underground parking garage and out into bright sunlight. The second that warmth brushes my face I roll the windows down and breathe in deeply. The sun feels better than it ever has, and the idea that I could lose it leaves me cold. I can't let them turn me. I shouldn't have made another deal with Adrian. The guys will kill me if they find out what I'm doing. I know Seth is my leader and he wants me to work with Adrian, but we never talked about it going this far. He doesn't know what I've asked.

And if Felix finds out--I don't want to know what he'd do.

The day is getting away from me, but I think back to everything so far. I feel old, but I know I'm not. Nineteen is nothing, but it's also everything. I started the day with a lovely breakfast with my mom at our favorite diner, and it was amazing. I have her back, and I still haven't processed it. Everytime I think of her actually being *her*, tears burn my vision.

Even now.

I wipe them away. I have to drive over to Felix and Seth's house. It's near the Tulane campus which is only a few miles up from the casino. Unfortunately, the drive through New Orleans is lovely but doesn't provide enough time to think of a plausible explanation for why I'm driving a Porsche. I've already forgotten what model Kelly said it is, so I'll just have to call it The Porsche.

I end up parking it down the road a little so I can walk over to Felix's place and allow the guys to assume I took the city bus here. I'm still not sure what Felix has in mind for my birthday date, but I'm super excited. We haven't had one-on-one time all week, and I need this. I'm still unsure if we're a real couple, though, considering we're hiding our relationship from Seth. That bothers me, but I agree with Felix. It's a necessity. Seth is our team leader and insists that dating between teammates should be off limits. And normally I'd agree with him, but Seth doesn't understand my heart or my history with Felix. I've been wanting this forever, and now that Felix finally wants it too, nothing is going to stop us.

I smile to myself. This secret can be sexy and fun if we let it. We'll tell everyone eventually, but for now, it's safer to keep it between the two of us. I knock on the door, and Felix opens it, takes my hand, and pulls me inside with a conspiratorial smile.

CHAPTER 5

"Surprise!" A chorus of voices crash over me, and I step back, momentarily stunned. Streamers in various shades of blue are ribboned across the tiny living room and helium balloons float in bunches.

I take it all in with a laugh. "Are you kidding me? You planned a surprise party?" I've never had one before.

Felix wraps me in a hug and whispers, "Happy birthday. There's someone here to see you." Then he turns me around and standing there in a blue party dress that matches her vibrant curly hair is none other than my best friend in the whole wide world.

"Ayla!" I scream, launching myself at her. I practically tackle her with my hug, and she hugs me back just as tight. "Oh my gosh, I've missed you so much," I gush. The last month has been the longest we've ever been apart since she up and moved on me to become a college girl.

"You have no idea," she replies in a tone that says *we need to talk.*

There are other people at this surprise party, like Seth and Kenton, my two new roommates, and a handful of people I have yet to meet who I'm guessing often come over to this house to hang out with their college friends. Some of these guys are built like they're definitely on the lacrosse team, too. But none of them really matter to me right now, not even Felix. All I want to do is talk with Ayla. Something is going on with my girl, and I have to know what it is.

"Later," she whispers, sensing exactly what I'm thinking. "Please, let's try to have fun."

And with that request, I do as she asks over the next couple of hours. Felix has set up a couple of drinking games, karaoke, and even got one of those massive sheet cakes from Costco. I don't drink and neither does my team, but I play along with everything else and end up having a great time. When they sing to me, I want to simultaneously crawl into a hole and hug everyone. After things settle down and I've met all the new people, Ayla and I finally get a chance to talk. I'm worried she's going to call me out on the sexual tension between me and her brother, and I feel bad keeping a secret from her. But maybe she hasn't sensed anything? Felix and I stayed apart most of the evening and Ayla took credit for the party. And maybe it really was all her idea, but I have a feeling that's not entirely true.

Arm in arm, we go up to Felix's room. It feels a little weird because I didn't think the first time I'd be up here would be with her, but I don't say that. The fact that she still doesn't know we've kissed is killing me. She's my person. But I'm not even sure what I am to Felix, so I pretend not to be extra interested in the posters on the wall or all the study materials on the desk as I sit down on the bed with her. What will she do when I tell her I've started something with her brother? I send a little prayer up that she'll support us, and I'm not even the praying type. Mom always said church wasn't her thing, though my grandma sometimes took me when I was a kid on the major holidays. Beyond that, I don't have much belief in a higher power. Especially one that would let vampires roam the earth.

I turn on my friend with a huge conspiratorial grin. "What are you doing here? And don't tell me you only came for the day because we both know a Sunday afternoon in September isn't really feasible for you to leave college. You're supposed to be long gone and having the best time of your life."

"Am I?" she teases, but she won't meet my eyes. I can sense the emotional wall she's built around herself, something that I've never experienced with my best friend before. She's always let me in. But then again, it's not like I'm one to talk …

"So, are you going to skip class for a few days or something?" I venture.

She sighs and tugs her hair behind her ear. It's greasy, which isn't like her either. Neither are the dark circles under her eyes.

"Listen, don't judge me okay?" Her eyes go round, and I grab her hands and squeeze. She returns the gesture but her grip is weak.

"I would never," I whisper.

"I know, but I also know how excited you were for me and everything, and I don't really know how to say this, so I'm just going to say it," she rushes. "I decided to drop out of school."

I squeeze her hands again, but she lets go. "Are you serious?" I wish I could do something to help her. This is the last thing I was expecting her to say––she was so excited to go.

"Yeah, I really hated it. I've never been so depressed in my entire life."

"I'm so sorry." I don't know what else to say. It's barely been a month.

"It's okay. Mom and dad support me coming home, at least for now. I went to a therapist and she said that a lot of kids get depression their first year of college and it can be really unhealthy for them." Her mouth wobbles and those round eyes fill with tears. "I guess I'm not as strong as I thought I was, huh?"

"Are you kidding me?" I want to shake her. "You're so

strong. Admitting something was wrong and taking action on that was super brave."

"Thanks." She shrugs. "Anyway, I'm going to stay home until I figure out what I want to do next. It's not like I need a college degree to do interior design at my own family's business, you know? But I'm not even sure I want to do interior design anymore. I'm not really sure about anything."

When I say my friend has been obsessed with home design since she was in preschool, I am not exaggerating. Her Sims houses are unbelievable, and her bedroom has changed about ten times over the years, each time better than the last. She was the kind of kid who asked for new bedding for her birthday instead of toys and rearranged furniture for fun. To this day she loves nothing more than to walk around IKEA and critique the displays. She's a total natural at this stuff, and to think that she'd give it up so quickly breaks my heart.

I wrap her in the tightest hug, wishing she would've confided in me about this sooner, but I am not about to make this about me. And it's not like I've been the world's greatest friend lately. So much has changed in my life, too. "I'm really sorry, Ayla. I know how much you were looking forward to your college experience. Are you sure this is the right decision?"

She pulls away and shoots me an annoyed glare. "You sound like Felix. He doesn't get it either. But honestly, I hated college. I never even wanted to leave my dorm room."

I nod, but I don't think she didn't want to leave her room because of being away from home or being shy or life changes or anything like that. I think the reason she wanted to stay locked up in her room was because she felt safe there and nowhere else. But I don't say that. Could my friend be going through post traumatic stress disorder after the vampire attack? Those guys had almost murdered her, and then we killed three of them right in front of her while she was still processing almost being vampire food. Not everyone is cut out to be a hunter, and my sensitive bestie might be hiding her true fears.

She stands. "I'm gonna head home before it gets dark. Happy birthday."

And sure enough, the sky outside has turned to bright creamsicle orange. She doesn't give me a present or a card, she simply leaves. It's not like I'm expecting a gift or that I'm mad that she didn't have something. It's that I'm even more concerned because this is not like her at all. My friend has always known I don't have much, so she goes all-out with her gifts. One time she even redid my wardrobe, saving up money meant for herself to use on new school clothes for me. And when I hadn't wanted to accept such a big gift, she'd already removed all the tags.

That's my Ayla. But I guess so is this girl. And I have no idea what to do.

Felix taps on the door and peeks inside. "Are you doing okay?"

I fake a happy smile. "Of course, thank you for this party. I know Ayla helped but you were the mastermind, weren't you?"

"I'll never tell." He winks and sits down next to me. "I have something for you."

He pulls a little box from the drawer of his nightstand. It's wrapped in blue paper to match the decorations downstairs. If I had to guess, Alya set him up with all of the party decor, which gives me some hope for my friend. But then again, maybe not. Maybe it was all him.

"Open it," he says, handing it over. I do and find a solid silver chain tucked neatly on top of a black velvet pillow inside.

"I saw that you broke the chain of your favorite necklace and had to replace it with something cheap," he says, his gaze dropping to my neck, "you know, the one that you wear all the time with the cross your grandmother gave you? Well anyway, I hope you like this replacement."

"It's one of the most thoughtful gifts anyone has ever given me," I breathe. Sure, driving a Porsche over here was one of the most surreal moments of my life. It's beautiful and brand new, and I'm still not sure why Adrian gave it to me . . . and I can't trust it. "Thank you so much, Felix. This is perfect." I've been wearing my cross on a crappy chain since Hugo broke it. It rests below my collarbone in its usual spot, half the time under my clothes. I pull it off to switch it out with the nice silver chain, and Felix clasps it to my neck for me.

As he does, my thumb glides along the stamped insignia of two tiny feathers crossing over each other on the back of the cross. The stamp belongs to the artisan who made it, a signature of sorts.

I turn back to him, and the energy between us completely shifts. His eyes flick to my lips, and before I can think about the consequences, I'm pressing my mouth to his. My senses have grown so much since having vampire venom in my blood, and even more since seeing Adrian, and it immediately kicks in with the kiss. I feel and hear and sense everything deeper than I ever have before––the hum of the ceiling fan, the warmth of Felix's soft mouth, the smell of his heady aftershave, the whoosh of my blood, and the swell in my breathing.

Maybe I'm not so mad about Adrian's orders to lose my virginity. My hands find a courage of their own, sneaking up under Felix's t-shirt to spread across his hard chest. He groans into my mouth. He tugs his shirt off, and then his hands are asking a question of their own. "This okay?" he whispers, tugging at my shirt as well. I nod against his kiss.

"Are you kidding me?" Ayla's voice breaks us apart like a bucket of ice water. She's standing in the doorway, her blue silhouette lit by the bright hallway behind her. And the look on her face is one of utter betrayal.

My heart drops.

"I can explain," I say at the same time Felix declares, "We were going to tell you."

"Don't bother," she snaps, and then she's gone before we can see her cry.

CHAPTER 6

"*T*hat went well," Felix grumbles as he slips his shirt back on. "I'd better go after her."

"I'll come with you."

But by the time we make it out to the front lawn, Ayla's nowhere to be seen. Felix runs to the sidewalk, peering up and down the street, his shoulders going limp. She probably parked around the corner because of the surprise party--I'd recognize her prized Mini Cooper anywhere--but there's no telling where that could be.

He stops abruptly. "Kenton, what are you doing?"

"Imagining myself in this sweet ride."

Kenton's voice sends a little nervous thrill through me. I rush over and, sure enough, my friend is standing next to my new car, staring at it like it's the most beautiful thing he's ever seen. Seth's got Kenton's phone out and is taking pictures of Kenton with the

Porsche like it's a display at an amusement park. From Seth's bored expression, this photoshoot was not his idea.

"Well, I guess now is as good a time as ever," I mutter. I tug the keys free from my pocket, dangling them for the guys to see. "Anyone want to take a ride?"

They gape at me.

"You told me you were taking the city bus here," Felix laments.

I look around to make sure it's only the four of us on the little tree-lined street. "And that was the plan, but you know how you want me to get in with the vampires?" At once, all of their expressions change. Seth looks concerned, Kenton impressed, and Felix down-right pissed off. "Well, Adrian agreed to keep working together and loaned me this car."

I leave out the fact that by "working together" I meant becoming his next *prodigy,* and that by "loan" I meant *give,* but hey, I'm working in baby steps here.

"Is it safe?" Felix asks as I unlock it. He's upon that car in all of two seconds flat, looking under the seats and in every nook and cranny like there's got to be a hidden camera or a bomb or something. "Can you pop the trunk? The hood too while you're at it."

Kenton and Seth are right there with him.

"Don't you think you're overreacting a bit?" I fold my arms over my chest and tap my foot on the pavement.

"No," Felix barks. His dark eyes land on mine from across the car. I'm not sure if he's mad that I took the gift or that Adrian gave the gift or what's going on exactly. Could it be jealousy?

"What if there's a tracking device on this thing?" Seth breaks my train of thought. "Or a camera or something worse?"

"What could be worse?"

"I don't know, a bomb?"

I laugh. "If Adrian wanted me dead, I'd be dead. Trust me."

"So what? You shouldn't have brought this here where your teammates live. You should've called me first and made a plan."

My cheeks warm. "Okay, you have a point," I relent, "I'm sorry." But what they don't realize is that if Adrian wanted to know who they were, then he wouldn't need to go to these lengths. He saw their faces that night behind the casino. He does his due diligence. It's very likely he already knows all about them. He could probably tell me their favorite breakfast cereal if I asked!

"Promise me one thing," Kenton says with a cheeky smile that breaks the tension. "Once we know it's safe, please let me be the first to drive her."

As it turns out, Kenton gets his wish. After about twenty minutes of investigating, they can't find a single thing wrong with the Porsche. Kenton and I climb in together for a joyride.

"But first, we need to set the tone," he says, connecting his phone to Bluetooth. He turns on one of my favorite hip hop albums and we take off. He goes right to the freeway. "We gotta see how fast this girl can go."

"Oh gosh, don't get us pulled over."

"I won't." He leans back in the driver's seat and tightens his grip on the wheel.

There's not a lot of traffic tonight, so he hits the gas and takes us up to the speed limit in seconds. I'm laughing the entire time.

Twenty minutes later we're back and Seth is next.

"Mind if I go alone?" he asks.

I shrug. "Go for it."

The request is a little weird but not unlike Seth, so whatever. Kenton gives me a hug and goes back to the party. I stay on the sidewalk with Felix. I'm not sure what to do. Hold his hand? Kiss him? Stay away because Ayla's obviously unhappy about us being together?

He calms my worries by wrapping me into a tight hug and kissing the top of my head. "It'll be alright," he says.

We stay like that until Seth returns a couple minutes later. As soon as we hear the car coming, we break apart. Seth doesn't need to know about us just yet. He parks and hands me the keys. I smile at Felix, dangling them in front of him.

"You ready?" I'm interested to know what he thinks about the car and to have another moment alone with him. "We can go together." And maybe we can go somewhere pretty even though the sun has already set. It's flat in New Orleans but there's got to be somewhere we can see the lights of the city. Or even just drive around for a while and talk. That would be nice. Ayla and I did that all the time when she first got her license.

"Sorry, I've got to get some homework done and we have training tomorrow, so I'd better not. Go enjoy your party though. It's all for you." He leaves me standing on the street, wondering what happened as he goes back inside with Seth. I want to go after him and demand . . . something.

But what?

It's only ten o'clock on my birthday, and I'm not ready for this day to be over. Everything has become so intense lately that getting this car and having some fun have felt like a dream. At least Kenton and I had a good time, but I wanted to experience it with Felix, and my feelings are a little hurt. I decide not to stick around the house any longer even though the party seems to be taking off again. I feel weird hanging out with a bunch of college kids when Felix is done for the night, so I say goodbye to everyone and check to see if my roommates want a ride home, but they don't. They're fun girls, and nice to me, but they're older and focused on school. I get the feeling that I'll never really get in with them, not the way real friends can. Not like with Ayla.

I slide into the driver's seat and retrieve my phone, wanting to call her. I call my mom instead. She picks up after the first ring. "Hi, Evangeline. How's my birthday girl doing?"

Mom's been staying with a work friend on the

outside of town since we got evicted, so getting to see her this morning was really nice. Ending the day in my own apartment instead of somewhere we live together? It's . . . weird. Not bad. Not good. Just—weird.

"I'm doing good, Mom." She still doesn't know much about my involvement with Adrian, and she definitely doesn't need to know about the Porsche, so I decide to leave that out.

She pauses for a second. "There's something I've been wanting to tell you."

I don't know if I've ever heard those words come out of her mouth. I sit up straight as my heart speeds up. "Why didn't you tell me at breakfast?"

"I didn't want to worry you on your birthday."

"Worry . . . are you kidding me? It's still my birthday, Mom." I roll my eyes. This is typical Virginia Blackwood, so I guess I shouldn't be surprised. At least she's not arguing with me about her gambling anymore. I hope we never have to talk about that again.

"Can I come by before your shift at Pops tomorrow? What time are you working?" Her voice is relaxed, which is not like her either. But maybe I haven't known the real her in a long time. She's probably going to be a lot different now that she's been compelled never to become addicted again, and I can't wait to get to know the person she is without all that, but I have to remind myself she's still Virginia. And she's never going to be perfect. Nobody is. And I'm okay with that.

I tell her when to meet me and we finish up talking

as I drive over to Ayla's house. If my best friend isn't ready to talk, I'll go home, but I can't end this day knowing I've hurt her. I need to make this right, so I park out front and knock on the same front door that I've knocked on a million times before.

Mrs. Moreno lets me in. "Honey, it's so good to see you." She hugs me right away.

"Can I see Ayla?"

She steps back with a little frown and whispers, "I hope you can get through to her. She's in her room."

Which is actually a guest room now. Ayla already helped her mom convert it to something new when she took most of her stuff to school. My heart does a little pang. Nothing went as planned. I wonder how she feels about everything. But maybe she's right, maybe she doesn't need a degree. Maybe college isn't for her. Maybe I'm completely off base about why she left.

I find her laying in bed with all the lights on and her laptop opened beside her. She's streaming an old sitcom with a terrible laugh track and doesn't acknowledge me when I come in and say hello. I sit on the edge of the bed for about five minutes and she doesn't move a muscle or look up once. When the audience members on the show laugh, she doesn't join them. "Are you really going to pretend like I'm not even here?" I finally ask.

"Sure am. Same as you pretended like I wasn't there anymore."

Yeah, we fight every now and then, but this seems pretty childish. And Ayla knows I've always had a thing for Felix. She didn't like it, didn't think anything would ever come of it, but she still knew and it's not like she ever seriously told me to stop. "I've called or texted you almost every day since you've been gone," I say.

"Yeah, and during all that you never once mentioned that you've been hooking up with my brother." She glares up from her computer. "How long has that been going on? Were you waiting for me to leave so you could shoot your shot?"

I hold up my hands. "First of all, I'm not hooking up with him. We've only kissed a few times. And second of all, you know I've always had a thing for your brother."

"Yeah, and I was cool with it because I thought you'd never act on it and that you'd always put our friendship first. You're *my* best friend, not *his* girlfriend."

"Why can't I be both?" I'm trying to hold my anger down, but she's not making it easy.

"Are you really asking me that?"

"Why wouldn't I be? You're being unfair."

"Because, Eva, if you date him, what happens when you break up? It'll force me to pick a side, and as much as I love you, he's *Felix*. I can't not pick my only sibling."

That hurts. She's already assuming Felix won't want me and is planning for a dramatic breakup. "You don't think I haven't thought about that?" I whisper. "I know you'd pick him, and do you realize how much that sucks for me? Because I *don't* have a sibling or another best friend. I have you. That's it."

"Apparently you have Felix."

I clench and unclench my fists, growing more and more frustrated. "Don't twist my words." We go quiet for so long that I'm forced to fill it. "I'm sorry, okay? I didn't mean for you to find out like that. This thing with Felix is brand-new."

"He had his shirt off. I'm not stupid, okay? So, did you finally lose your virginity then?"

I stand up, growing exhausted by this argument. "No, and even if I did, it shouldn't be such a big deal. A girl shouldn't be defined by her decisions about her body."

"Are you kidding? It's a big deal because you've always made it a big deal. I know what it means to you."

"Okay but--"

"And it's a big deal when it's your best friend who's keeping secrets from you."

Silence stretches between us, pulling us further and further apart. "You don't understand," I grumble.

"You're right, I don't."

"Ayla--"

"I think you should leave."

And I think maybe she's right. I go to stand in the doorway. I'm burning mad, but I also understand where she's coming from because I know her better than anyone, and I know she was already hurting when she came home and now I've added to that pain with my secrets. I wonder if this is less about Felix and more about me keeping something from her. "Please, get help, okay? You need someone to talk to about everything.

Are you going to be seeing that therapist regularly now?"

"So you think that because I dropped out of school that I'm somehow defective? Well, at least I tried, Eva. I don't see you trying."

"That stings." My voice goes low. She knows how I was brought up, and she certainly knows I'm doing my best. I wasn't raised like her with two parents, a steady income household, a beautiful house to grow up in, a legacy and cultural traditions and, and, and . . . I take a deep breath. "I'm actually talking about the vampire attack last month. You haven't been the same since that awful party. You're attributing your unhappiness with going away to college, but I just want you to talk to someone who can help you separate the two because maybe it's the vampire thing that's got you feeling this way. A professional is trained to help you get closure on things like that."

"Closure?" She rolls her eyes. "How am I supposed to get closure when suckers are still out there? And now I have to think about you and Felix going out and hunting them every night when you're not doing God knows what else."

"Not every night." In fact, we haven't even gone out on a first official mission. Tate still isn't back. Cameron is running the show like the little twerp he is, and he hasn't authorized our team to actually do anything but train. We can't even drop stakes in graveyards right now because the last time the guys did that, they went at night when they weren't supposed to. It was the night I followed them and got attacked by a newly turned vampire, but I don't think Cameron knows anything about that.

"Hunting is our way of coping with this messed up world," I say at last, "you need to find your way of coping too."

"Can you go now?" She's being mean, and I could serve it right back, but I'm tired and I don't want to fight. Hopefully she'll soften over time and forgive me. But I'm not going to stop seeing Felix now that I've started. And I'm not going to give up the hunters. And I'm certainly not going to give up on Ayla's mental health or our friendship.

"You know," she says right before I close the door. "It's best if you don't come around here anymore. It's safer for me considering your questionable life decisions."

Tears prickle in my eyes, and I don't know what to do or say because she's right. She might not be safe around me. It's the reason I didn't stay here when the Morenos' offered after Mom and I got evicted. And that was a good decision considering Hugo had me followed, and that Adrian knew the details of my home's layout and where I slept. Who's to say other vamps aren't after me? And now that I'm actually Adrian's fledgling, I'm going to have even more eyes on me.

I close the door and refuse to cry.

On the way out of the house, I give her parents a hug.

"Contact me if you ever need anything or if Ayla needs me."

Their eyes widen in surprise but they nod their agreement. I leave before they can start asking questions. I really hope Ayla will come around to my way of thinking or at least forgive me soon. But I'm not so sure she will. I know my friend––she's as stubborn as I am.

CHAPTER 7

"Guess who's back?" Kenton greets me as I amble into the gym the next morning after a terrible night's sleep. At first, I'm confused by the statement, but then I see *him*--Leslie Tate. He's standing on the stairs chatting with a few of the other hunters. The older man looks the same as he always did with his gray, inquisitive eyes hooded by bushy eyebrows. He was only gone for a few weeks, but to me it feels like an eternity. It also feels like something is wrong.

"Well, what did he say?" I remove my hoodie and toss it into one of the cubbies, heading over to the weights area with Kenton at my side. We've fallen into a routine where we workout together in the mornings. First we spot each other, then we spar. Felix and Seth are already out on the mat, paired up for the same thing. Once we're all done, we have to do some of the simulations upstairs, maybe a lecture or two, and then we're out before lunch. I know the guys are chomping at the bit to get real assignments, but I'm starting to get a little nervous about the prospect of actually hunting.

"What do you mean what did he say?" Kenton asks, genuinely confused by my question.

I widen my eyes. "Oh, I don't know, maybe about the fact that he ditched us, only leaving behind a cryptic note like we're all in some kind of murder mystery novel?"

Kenton shrugs. "Didn't think to ask."

"Right . . ."

He changes the subject, and we go about our training. The craziest part is that everyone I talk to about Tate throughout the morning gives me a similar answer. They don't seem to care where their leader has been or why he left, only that he's back. Surely Tate isn't infallible to scrutiny. Do they follow this man blindly no matter what?

I corner Cameron by the drinking fountain. We're alone so I need to be quick. "Hey, do you know what's going on? Everyone's acting like it's no big deal that Tate is back."

"Why don't you talk to Tate yourself?" Cameron says, shooting me an odd look. "That's what I did."

"Uhh––what about the whole energy demon thing?"

"The what?" Cameron raises his eyebrows. They're bushy today, reminding me of orange caterpillars.

"You know." I make sure nobody is around us and

then whisper low. "The whole reason why you're a prodigy for Kelly."

Cameron steps back, his face going slack. "I don't know what the hell you're talking about. What's your name again? Aren't you a novice?"

Huh? "Eva, and yes, but that's not the point. I'm talking about the nightclub and Kelly. Remember when we were at the casino and––"

He shakes his head, holding up his hands. "Alright, Ava. I don't know what you're trying to do here, but whatever it is, you need to stop."

"It's Eva."

"Whatever. Don't make up lies like that."

I open and close my mouth a few times. "But what about your little brother? Avenging his death and all that *if you can't beat them, join them* stuff?"

Cameron's face pales. "My brother died of childhood cancer." His voice is dangerously low, like he's close to erupting. I catch sight of his clenched hands and step back. "And what are you doing looking into me like that? I don't even know you. Are you doing this to everyone?"

I stare at him, completely flabbergasted. Did he really forget everything? It's hard to believe, but then I know what Tate can do. He told me from day one that he can make people forget things. Has he done that to me? My mind whirls with the possibilities, and suddenly I want to run far, far away from this secret training facility and never look back.

But my friends are here and I can't leave them vulnerable.

"Everything okay here?" Seth slides in next to me. He assesses Cameron with a hard stare.

"Is this girl on your team?" Cameron asks. He's short and stocky, but his bulk is considerable and his hands are fisted.

"Yes." Seth's tone darkens to match Cameron's, and I'm grateful that Seth decided to get over his annoyance and welcome me to his team. It feels good to be wanted. It's not a feeling I've had too many times before.

"Your little girl here is digging into people's backgrounds, and you need to get her to stop."

Seth turns to me. "Is this true?"

I don't know what to say to get this to make sense, but my team knows about Cameron, who he really is and what his plans are. At least, what they were before his mind was washed clean like a window. In the end, I decide to go with Cameron's side of things just to get him to leave us alone. "Yeah, I guess so. Sorry about that, Cameron. It won't happen again."

Cameron huffs and stalks off, his eyes still on me as he crosses the gym to join his teammates.

"Okay, so what was that really all about?" Seth is never that interested in me, but right now he's looking at me with scrutinizing eyes. There is also sympathy in them. And trust. And I love that he trusts me. I didn't realize how much I needed it.

"You still remember the stuff I told you about Cameron before, right?" I whisper.

"Yes."

Relief floods through me. "Good, because the guy was just acting like he had no recollection of any of it."

"Nothing? Do you think he was bullshitting you?"

"Could be, but I really don't think so. His memory was wiped."

"Hmm . . ." Seth turns, and we both watch Cameron as he starts to spar with one of his teammates. They're not in the gym a lot because they're usually out hunting, but today it's like everyone's here. Maybe Tate told the leaders to call all their teammates in.

"I asked him about Leslie Tate, and he acted like it's no big deal that Tate is back. Same with Kenton. Do you think something's going on?"

Seth's eyes go from hard to soft. "Nothing's wrong. You can trust Tate. Go talk to him yourself and see."

"Well, Tate obviously wiped Cameron's mind, so you'll excuse me if I don't want to talk to the guy."

"Nah, trust me, Tate is a good guy. If he did anything weird, he did it to protect us."

Okay, so now Seth is acting the same way as everyone else, and I am certain something is definitely up with Tate. Maybe I should stay away, but it feels inevitable. Against my better judgement, I take to the stairs, determined to get answers.

I find Tate in his office, sitting at his desk, business as usual.

"Hi, Eva," he greets me with a smile. "How are you doing?"

I sit down in the chair across from him and glower. "I'm fine. More interesting question––how are *you* doing? And while you're at it, where have you been? And why did you ditch us like that?"

Tate nods once, understanding framing his eyes.

"And for that matter, what happened to Cameron? He's wiped. You took his memories away, I know you did."

"I helped Cameron." He leans forward. "Do I need to help you?"

Does he know about Adrian? I blink and my heart speeds up.

"All your questions are valid." He smiles. "But they're questions you don't need to ask or think about anymore."

There's something about his words that sink into me like an anchor. He's telling the truth. Even if there's something about that truth that's not entirely ringing true, it's still trustworthy. I try to grasp on to what could be off about this moment, but my mind goes a little fuzzy. I need to remember that he's doing something to me, that he's using his powers somehow. I need to cling to the fact that he himself admitted to being something other than human the first time we met. I need to hold on to Cameron's words at the nightclub, that Tate is some kind of energy demon, and I need, I need . . .

The fuzziness takes over my thoughts and then clears, leaving nothing behind.

"Okay," I say simply. My mind is at ease, so I get up to leave. "When will we be resuming training together?" He takes new recruits under his wing, and I've really missed having that one on one time with him. He's a great guy, like the father I never had.

"How about tomorrow?"

A little burst of happiness releases in my chest. "I'll be here."

Felix wraps me in his arms and kisses me one last time. "It's been fun having you around today."

I smile and nod. We're standing on his front porch after having spent most of our Monday together. After practice this morning, he apologized for turning in early last night, and asked me to hang out at his house in between his classes so he could hop over and spend time with me. Since I wasn't working until later, I figured it was a good idea. And I'd been right. The whole day was amazing, so much so that I think I'm almost ready to take Adrian up on his request and finally cash in my v-card with Felix. Not today because I've got to get to work, but soon.

We hug and then I reluctantly walk down to my car. Whatever jealousy Felix had about the Porsche, he hasn't said another word about it. Maybe he realized he was being a jerk.

I wave goodbye and slide in, then pull out on the road and turn toward downtown. I have to go home and change into my work uniform, and I'm keenly aware that my mom wanted to swing by first to talk to me about something. I'm super curious about whatever it is she wants to tell me––and nervous. I didn't like the tone of her voice, it reminded me too much of the days before Adrian compelled her.

As I turn the corner, I catch sight of Tate walking through a parking lot. Seeing him out in the wild like this makes me pause at the stop sign and watch him. I shouldn't worry about what he's doing, but something deep within warns that's a false thought. I'm filled with mixed emotions, but I follow that little warning bell, pulling into the same parking lot. I jog over to the side-walk to catch up with him, but he doesn't see me in time and walks into a revolving door before I get a chance to call out his name.

I want to say hi and to thank him for coming back after he had left and ask . . .

There's something else, something important, but my mind has gone fuzzy again. I don't know if it's out of curiosity or a suspicion I can't quite name, but I find myself following Tate inside the building.

I look up at the sign above the glass door and frown a little: Tulane Medical Center. What could he be doing at a hospital? I hope he's okay. My first thought is he's probably visiting someone and would appreciate his privacy. But my feet keep moving forward, and I walk right past reception, following him to an unmarked door. I find myself in a plain hallway, Tate's footsteps echoing ahead. Again, I want to call out to him, but a deep sense of knowing crawls up my throat. It seals my mouth shut, and all I can do is follow him.

CHAPTER 8

Once again, my senses grow, everything prickling to keen awareness. The scent of anti-septic, the clacking of shoes on polished tiles, and the air conditioning running through the vents all seem to surround me at once. I'm not sure why it's so strong right now because Tate isn't a vampire or connected into Hugo's bloodline. Maybe it's because I'm sensing something is off or because I'm hyper-focused. I'm still not sure how this venom works yet, but I'm certain that I have to keep it a secret. The vampires will kill me if they find out I have it. Adrian still might. And I don't want Tate to know.

Pieces of my mind still want to relax and let Tate go, but clarity has peeked through like sunbeams in thick clouds. Clarity that says, *it's time to learn the truth about Tate.* I grit my teeth, realizing the only reason why I want to trust Tate is because he *told* me to, and that has more to do with his secret abilities than it does with how I actually feel deep down. I've been manipulated, plain and simple.

Growing angry, I push through double doors and end up inside a bustling emergency room floor. I wouldn't have known how to get back here without asking at reception, and I find it odd that Tate did. What's a guy like him doing sneaking around a hospital? If he were visiting someone, there wouldn't be a need for secrecy.

A middle-aged woman with blurry red eyes rushes past, and I catch sight of the bright blue visitor sticker on her shirt. I fold in on myself, hoping nobody will notice that I don't have one of my own. What I'm doing might be illegal, but luckily the place is busy, and it seems the doctors and nurses aren't concerned with me, not when they have ten places to be at once. A sign at the far end of the hall reads *Blood Donation Center*, and I recoil. I shouldn't, it probably has nothing to do with feeding vampires and everything to do with saving humans, but I'm turned off by any kind of blood donation at this point. There's a reason the top ailments in our society have become anemia, restless leg syndrome, fatigue, brain fog, and more—all symptoms of donating too much blood.

I've lost sight of Tate and can't very well start opening doors to look for him, so instead I casually stroll down the hall, keeping my eyes open. I've never had to be admitted into an ER before, but I did bring Mom into one once when she donated too much blood, and I know hospitals well enough from when my gran died. I've avoided those memories, but being here now makes me think that maybe it wouldn't be such a bad idea to go into medicine. I've always wanted to help people, and since being a police officer turned out to be a bust, maybe I could go to nursing school or do something in the medical field. I like the buzz of this ER and the thought of responding to people in immediate need. Maybe I could find my way into working here and keep hunting vampires on the side, at least until my brain fully develops and it's no longer safe to be near vampires.

The idea seems . . . impossible.

But maybe it's not.

There's a huge glass door marked ICU for Intensive Care Unit in bright red lettering. The unit inside is surrounded in glass and lit with sunshine, as if all that light helps the people in there heal. I peek through the glass, my breath catching when I spot Tate. He's standing with his back to me next to someone in a hospital bed. The patient has so many tubes and wires taped to him that I can barely make out his face. Whatever is going on with this guy, it looks like it's pretty bad.

Something catches the light, and I blink rapidly and

then squint. Just like that night at the Neon House, the humans have auras again. This time I don't need neon to see the energy––I can see it in broad daylight––another sense heightened. They're all sorts of colors, but the person lying on the bed has a very weak yellow glow around them, and exactly like Cameron claimed, Leslie Tate is syphoning the energy away from the human. It flows from the person in the bed directly into Tate's body.

I have to run in there, to rip him away from that innocent person, but when I yank on the glass door, it doesn't budge. I curse, realizing it's because I don't have access. I really don't understand how Tate got inside because surely he doesn't have access either. It's like the man went to a hospital looking for the person in the weakest state and zeroed in on them. It's horrific. Cameron was right. If I don't stop him, Tate's going to kill that guy.

I bang on the glass door, but nobody inside hears me, and Tate doesn't stop or even flinch in my direction. Is that why they come here––these energy vampires/demons––to prey on humans at their very weakest? Do they get some kind of extra boost when they take a life? Is that why Cameron's brother was targeted?

"Stop!" I yell.

"Excuse me, you can't go back there," a nurse cuts me off sharply.

I turn to her, panic growing. "See that man?" I point

to Tate. "He's hurting your patient."

Her eyebrows furrow and then she's through the door, closing it in my face before I can follow after her. I expect her to stop him, but as she approaches Tate, her body language softens, all urgency evaporating into thin air. She doesn't even bother to speak to him. In fact, she moves past the patient and Tate as if he's not even there, as if the patient is completely fine and peacefully dreaming about sugar plum fairies.

"Are you kidding me?" I hiss, looking around the hallway for someone else who could get me access into the ICU.

This must be part of why his kind—whatever they are—have gone undetected for so long. Nobody can stop them because the second a human questions them, they're able to turn our minds to peach fuzz.

I can fight it, but that must be because of the venom.

I still don't agree with Cameron's whole "if you can't beat them, join them" attitude, but I can understand why he's so concerned about these things, why he made it his life's mission to stop them after the things he witnessed. I make a mental note to grill Adrian about these *things* next time I see him because surely he knows. This must be why he wants me to spy on Tate for him, so I can give him more information on his enemy. This is far beyond humans hunting down vampires. Maybe the vampires don't fear human hunters at all, maybe it's these *other things* that are the true targets.

My mind whirls with the implications, and questions

sprout in my mind. What if it's not only humans in that gym every morning? What if there are others like Tate working with us? How many are out there like him? Could Seth or Kenton be one of them?

I used to think I knew everything. I've since realized I know nothing.

I turn around and spot a grumpy looking security officer charging right toward me. Maybe banging on an ICU door wasn't the best way to keep myself inconspicuous. Not my smartest idea, I'll admit. I take on a relaxed posture and walk briskly in the opposite direction. He follows, but before he can get to me, I'm strolling through the waiting room, and then I'm on the front sidewalk, and then I'm sprinting back to the Porsche.

I jump in and peel out of the parking lot, my heart rioting in my chest.

Maybe there was nothing I could do to help that one person in the ICU, and it kills me to even think about leaving them vulnerable like that, but now I know that Cameron was right about one thing: there's definitely more out there than vampires. And maybe he's right that vampires aren't the worst of them. That's hard to believe with what I know of the suckers, but at least they're out in public and open about their vileness. At least they have weaknesses, like the sun and silver and wood through the heart. And at least they don't lie about who they are.

Because Tate is a liar. And now I really want to know

where he disappeared to and why. I drive home with my knuckles white on the steering wheel and more questions than ever racing through my head.

CHAPTER 9

I lean against the side of the brick wall, aimlessly watching the cars in the street and the people on the sidewalk. I have to go into work but I've been standing out here in the evening sun waiting for someone who will never come.

My mom stood me up.

And even though she's done it a million different times before, this one stings the most. It's my own fault for caring so much. I'd dropped my guard and allowed myself to hope. I shouldn't have done that. I know better, have *learned* better. Experience is the best teacher, as they say. I hate that I was foolish enough to let this happen.

Because hope is cruel. It rips your heart out. It breaks promises and doesn't return phone calls and treats you like an afterthought and makes you late for work.

I was stupid to trust her again. All it took was one

conversation with her, one happy birthday breakfast, one promise that things were going to be different this time, that she was better, that it was impossible for her to be sick again.

Adrian obviously didn't compel her to be a better mom, and it's sad that I wish he had.

And as I march into Pops, pissed off and ten minutes late for my shift, all I can think is that I should've refused to celebrate my birthday altogether. That would've been my preference! That's what I had wanted. I'd been content with not celebrating in any way, shape, or form. As the day had approached, I had not allowed myself to think of it. Why should I? I didn't want to grow older, and I certainly didn't want to be disappointed. It was always better to set expectations low because that way nobody could hurt me.

"You okay?" Eddie frowns when he sees me. I assumed he would give me a stern talking to about being late, but maybe he caught the expression on my face because he only seems concerned. I don't really get it. I'm here to do a job. This is the second time I've messed up. First, I had called in with an emergency and had no coverage, and now, I was late and in a piss-poor mood.

"Yeah, I'm fine," I say. "Sorry I'm late."

He nods. "You're okay. Go clock in."

And that's it. He doesn't question me, which is exactly the slack I need right now in my tug-of-war life. Maybe it's another strike against professionalism, but I give him a big bear hug. I can hardly get my arms around him, but the man pats me on the back and tells me to take better care of myself. Maybe he can see the bags forming under my eyes from all the late nights and early mornings. Or maybe he can sense the stress I'm under, especially when it comes to worrying about my mom. Or the sadness from losing my best friend.

I go about my shift, and Eddie walks me to my car afterward. He raises an eyebrow when he sees the Porsche. I can't claim it as my own, I just can't. Maybe because of who really owns it, or maybe because I don't think I actually deserve it. I don't know. "It's a friend's car, not mine," I explain sheepishly, "he's letting me drive it for a while until I can get my own."

Eddie whistles low. "Some friend, huh?" I climb in, and he pats the roof. "Be careful, okay? Sometimes a gift isn't really for the giftee as much as the gifter, know what I'm saying?"

I nod, knowing exactly what he's saying and wishing I didn't.

"So then you have to ask yourself, is it really a gift?"

His words follow me the entire drive home, and when Mom texts apologizing and wanting to reschedule for a lunch date instead, I don't respond.

A week passes by, and I don't hear from her again. I don't hear from Adrian either. Or Ayla. I find myself hanging out at the guys' house more and more, which has become a little tricky for me and Felix. A few nights ago we agreed to be official, but we're still pretending to be just friends whenever Seth is around. And considering Seth is his roommate, that happens to be a lot.

"Alright, level with me," I say the next chance we have to be alone. We're sitting on the living room couch watching SportsCenter. I couldn't care less about sports, but I don't mind it since Felix enjoys it so much. But there's something I've been meaning to talk to him about. "Why have you been avoiding coming over to my apartment?"

Because that's the thing. We could be alone there any chance we wanted. But Felix keeps wanting to hang at his house, and I don't get it. I've thought about this a lot and I want to take things to the next step with him, but it's like he's pushing it off.

Felix tugs at the tips of his curly hair nervously and his cheeks go red. "Well, I guess it's because I used to hook up with Jasmine."

One sentence from those pretty lips of his and my world tilts off its axis.

He's referring to my roommate who I almost never see, the pretty Latina girl who's always at the library studying for her pre-med degree. I like her from the few interactions I've had with her, and she came to my birthday party, but I never expected to get this news. I sink into the couch and take it in. I guess I shouldn't be too surprised since Felix is a twenty-year-old college student. He's sexy as hell with his sleeve tattoo and that

Cuban ethnicity girls love around here. He's a star player on the lacrosse team so he's built like a model. And don't forget he's super smart and going into business, where he'll surely become the CEO of some Fortune 500 company one day. Sometimes I can't believe he wants me. He's got his life together. I don't.

"Well, I could see how that could be a problem." My throat goes dry.

"Her and I are just friends, I promise." He leans over to wrap me in a hug. "And I'm exclusive with you now."

Right. I want to believe him . . . I do believe him. The simple fact that he was the one who found me a room in her apartment is confirmation enough that he's not into her anymore. He wouldn't have done that if he had something to hide. He's helped me, been kind, looked out for me, and finally seen me as something other than a kid sister. This is everything I've been wanting for years. I can't screw this up.

"Well, we're alone now, aren't we?" I scoot in closer and run the tips of my fingers along the little curls at the back of his neck. "Why don't we go up to your room?"

There's no denying my meaning.

It takes more courage than I care to admit. Maybe it's because I've been holding onto my virginity for so long, or maybe it's because for so many years I fantasized it happening with Felix and nobody else, but I've been thinking about this a lot, and I think Adrian is right. At first I was angry at him for acting like he should get a say in what I do with my body, but I realize now that he's a logical creature and logic says I need to take care of this to be safer among the vampires. I don't know what my blood smells like to them. Even Kelly, who hates me, said I smell like the sweetest flower.

For some gross unexplainable reason, virgin blood smells better to vampires than nonvirgin blood. And now that I'm planning to be around vampires a lot more––who better to lose it with than the one guy I've pined over for ages?

Felix leans over and kisses me, long and slow and deep. Butterflies tickle through my stomach and my heart speeds up. I imagine that at any second he's going to scoop me into his arms and follow through with my request.

He doesn't.

He pulls back and stands. "I actually need to get to class."

My heart drops. I didn't know he had a class coming up. He never said so, and a little voice in my head says he's making up an excuse to get rid of me. I stand up, annoyed, and an angry fire rushes in to snuff out the insecurities.

"What's a girl got to do around here to lose her virginity, huh?" I throw my arms up.

Felix doubles over in laughter. I don't know what I expected Felix to do, but laughing? It makes me even angrier.

"Sorry." He tries to pull me into a hug, but I dodge him. "I don't mean to laugh at you."

"Sure," I deadpan.

He calms down. "You just reminded me of why I like you so much."

"Oh, you need reminding?" I put my hands on my hips and shoot him a glare.

"No, I don't." He turns serious. "But this isn't easy for me."

"And why is that?" Now I'm even more offended. I don't want to be some chore to him. "You've slept with loads of girls before. Do I repulse you or something?"

"No, Eva. You're the most tempting thing I've ever laid eyes on and I've thought so for a long time. But you're my sister's best friend, and she's mad as hell at me right now."

"She'll come around."

"Will she? I'm not so sure. Not to mention, you're on my hunter team, and my best friends are telling me to back off."

"I thought they didn't know about us."

"They're not stupid." He grins sheepishly. "They see the way we are together. And you have been hanging out here every day lately."

He makes good points, but I still don't care. This is about us, not everyone else. "Why are you letting other people dictate *your* life?"

The front door swings open, and, as if to mock me, Kenton and Seth bulldoze inside. "Who's hungry?" Kenton asks. "I'm ordering pizza."

"Actually, we were leaving," I reply.

"Together?" Seth questions, his tone accusatory.

"If you must know, your boy here claims to have a class coming up. And I have . . . things to do." I don't have things to do.

"I thought it was your night off?"

"Fine. If you must know, my thing to do was supposed to be Felix." I go to the door and turn back, giving all the guys my dirtiest glare. "And by the way, my dating life is my business. I'm a grown ass woman who can make her own choices."

Kenton yells at Felix, "Damn, son! What did you do?"

I leave, the door banging behind me. Seth follows me. Which, I gotta admit, only adds fuel to the fire. Felix should be out here, begging for my forgiveness, not Seth to rub it all in.

"Hold up, Eva," he calls after me, "I think we need to talk about this."

I spin on my heels. "Oh, you mean about how you've decided that you get a say in what goes on in *my* relationship?"

His face hardens. "This is to protect all of us." But there's something else in his meaning, and I can't quite put my finger on it.

"What aren't you telling me?"

Then Seth does something I've never seen him do-- he blushes.

And I know.

He looks away, and I drop it, because I'm not going to make him say it. *But I know.* All the signs are there.

The way he treats his friends, the way he acts around Felix, the attitude he gives me and how he's tried to push me away . . .

Seth is in love with Felix.

How did I not see it before? Does Felix know?

"Don't say anything." Seth's voice is raw with emotion. "Please."

I nod once. I would never out someone. I don't know Seth's reasons for staying closeted.

He runs his hand through his hair and shakes his head. "Look, I know I can't have him. I'm not stupid enough to think he's going to switch teams for me or anything like that. Guys like me? We've been in this situation before."

"Seth, I don't know what to say."

"It's fine. Whatever. But that doesn't mean I magically approve of your relationship because I don't."

"But Felix means as much to me as he does to you."

He holds my gaze. "I know, okay? I'm a hypocrite. And I'm sorry I haven't been the kindest to you. Now you know why. But that aside, the two of you dating is a horrible idea."

I shake my head. "Felix and I have known each other for years. We wouldn't get involved if we didn't really care about this working out. Don't you want him to be happy?"

"You really don't get it, do you?"

Pretty sure I do get it. He's jealous—to the point of ruining our happiness.

"I don't care about Felix's happiness," he says, practically reading my mind. "I care about his *life*. I want to keep him alive. And you. And all of us. Hunters aren't supposed to date each other, and there's good reasons for that. The vampires could use Felix against you. And don't think for one second that your buddy Adrian wouldn't do that, because he would."

He wouldn't.

Maybe he would.

"Go home," Seth continues, "think about it. Take your emotions out of the equation and really think this through using your brain and nothing else."

"I have."

"No, you haven't, because if you had you'd already be at the same conclusion." He sighs heavily and steps back. "I already know Felix is willing to risk everything on you, so he hasn't thought this through enough either." My heart does a little happy dance at his confession, despite what he's trying to say. All I want to do is go back in there, work things out with Felix, and then drag him up to his room and tell everyone else to stay out of our business.

Seth must see my thoughts written all over my face because his voice turns angry. "Are you honestly that selfish that you're willing to risk Felix's life? You think you know Adrian better than the rest of us, but don't forget what he is, and don't forget that you *don't* really know him. You can't."

"He's encouraged me to be with Felix, actually," I jut in. "He wants me to lose my virginity."

"So lose it with someone else!"

"Are you kidding me?"

"You just proved my point that your vampire already knows about Felix." His voice goes dark. "If it were between Adrian's life and yours, Adrian would choose his own, and he'd drink you dry to do it. Now imagine Felix mixed up in that. Imagine what it would feel like to have your boyfriend and your best friend's brother killed because of your choices. Choices that could be avoidable if you treated Felix like a teammate and kept things professional."

A tear burns down my cheek––one that I didn't even know was there until it brands me with the truth.

Because Seth is right.

My heart breaks, but I walk away without another word. I don't go back in there to work things out with Felix. I get into my car and go home to my apartment alone. After a few hours of thinking it all through, I send Felix a text asking for us to stick to being friends. When he calls me back immediately, I don't answer. And when he blows up my phone with texts, I don't respond to any of them. And even when he shows up at my doorstep later that night, begging to talk to me, I have my room-mate Olive send him away.

CHAPTER 10

*B*y the next morning, Felix gives up, and that hurts the most. I cry into my pillow and then I scream into it. Once that's done, I wipe the tears and sit up, phone in hand.

I need some time off, I text Seth. *I'll see you guys when I'm ready.*

So you're quitting?

Of course not, but I'm taking a short break.

Fine, but we need you by next Monday. We can't miss more than a week. I think we'll be getting assignments soon.

"Yeah, I'll believe it when I see it," I grumble out loud.

Going back to the gym at all seems like a huge chore, and honestly, I'm angry about everything. I'm angry about the guys, about Tate, and about being a hunter in general. Becoming one of them was supposed to be rewarding, and so far we haven't even been on a single mission. Seth may think we'll be sent out soon but I'm skeptical. We're training and learning, and we need time to get prepared so we don't end up dead. I have to keep reminding myself that it's only been a little over a month, and I'm not being very patient.

But I'm ready.

Hugo's venom has enhanced my senses, gaining strength each day and adding to my confidence that I could hunt down vampires with ease. This has nothing to do with simulations. This has to do with blood. I'm linked into their bloodline, which means that I can sense them better than anyone. And maybe if I accomplish what I set out to do, I won't feel so guilty about everything else.

It's too bad Tate can't be trusted. I've avoided him ever since seeing him in the ICU. If I could trust him then I'd tell him about the venom in my blood so he could send me out. I'd be able to help the mission. But then, who's mission? The humans or the energy demons? I'm confused and indecisive, which isn't like me. I'm not sure I like the person in the mirror these days.

Going to Adrian for help late Friday night is the last thing I ever thought I'd do, but the phrase "never say never" hits me right across the face as I walk into the Alabaster Heart Hotel and Casino uninvited.

Kelly sits at her office reception desk and doesn't seem surprised as I approach. She looks me up and down and smiles devilishly. "You didn't dress up."

"Hello to you, too." I look down at my high-waisted cut-off jeans and forest green baggy t-shirt, wondering what the big deal is. My little silver cross necklace is tucked under my shirt, and I've got my wooden stake strapped to my ribcage. I'm sure Adrian will notice, but at this point he'd probably find it more out of character if I didn't have one.

"I need to talk to Adrian."

Kelly stands on five inch heels and motions for me to follow. I expect her to lead me to the elevator, but she doesn't. We must be going to Adrian's suite, or maybe out on the casino floor, or even downstairs to the ballroom the coven uses for meetings.

I'm wrong on all counts because we cross the opulent lobby and go outside.

The sunset has given way to an inky black sky, the city lights blotting out the stars. The energy bustles around us with evening partiers, many of which are probably tourists. Even though it's known for having more vampires than a lot of cities, people still flock here. A group of intoxicated girls wobble past us on high heels, heading toward the nightclub across the street. I catch a whiff of booze mixed with a cloud of perfume and I grimace.

I wonder how many of the people in there have donated blood instead of paying a cover fee. They can't possibly feel safe. Why do people keep doing it, keep exchanging their safety for a night of fun? We follow them to the club. They go to the back of the line that

NINA WALKER

wraps around the block, but Kelly and I head right past the massive vampire bouncer.

The moment we step inside, I want to turn back around. Suckers are everywhere––behind the bar, in the seats, dancing on the floor. There are far more vamps in here than there are humans, but several of the humans have a nurse with them drawing blood. Opening a vein to gain free drinks for the night must be too good to pass up for many. Before I was around vampires, it wasn't always obvious what they were, but now that I know what to look for, it's impossible not to see them. It's a knowledge I wish I didn't have.

Canal Street separates the city, the old from the new, and we're on the newer side of town. It's all shiny black surfaces and purplish-red lights here, unlike the casino which has obviously been renovated but still clings to the old charm. Kelly leads me to the back of the club where a spiral metal staircase twists up to the top floor. Another bouncer lets us through to what must be the VIP area. We climb, and I become acutely aware of how underdressed I am.

"I need to talk to Adrian about something," I say, uneasy. "And then I can leave."

"Oh, did I forget to tell you?" She laughs. "You've been invited to a special coven meeting."

My face burns. "This is the first I'm hearing of it, and you know it."

"Too bad Adrian didn't give me a deadline to inform you about it," she muses, "but I'm telling you now."

She has to do as her master says, but she found a way to make it harder for me. I wonder how Adrian will respond when he finds out what she's done. "And what were you going to do if I didn't happen to walk into the casino tonight?"

She lifts a shoulder. "I know where you live."

"I moved."

She only laughs at that. Of course these suckers are going to keep tabs on me wherever I go. I'm not surprised that she knows about the new address, but my stomach hardens anyway.

"By the way," she goes on, "what's the deal with my fledgling? I went to pay him a visit last night and he practically tried to kill me."

"There's a reason for that and it's exactly why I want to talk to Adrian."

"I guess it's your lucky night." But her tone has darkened, and I wonder how important it is that she gets Cameron to follow through with his promises. Brisa loved the idea of having a hunter working on their side. If Kelly's lost that, Brisa won't be happy. Does Kelly know Cameron's already long gone?

"I don't think it's anyones lucky night," I mutter.

The top floor is two stories above the rest with a balcony looking over the dance floor. It's a little bit quieter up here, and less packed, with black velvet couches placed around the edges of the room. In the middle are three long metal poles. Dancers swing around them, their toned bodies moving to the music.

They aren't nude, they're in tiny bras and underwear, but once my eyes catch on Adrian, I can't look at anybody else.

And he's staring right back.

"Remember, Eva," Kelly whispers, "you're his now. This is what you wanted."

I brush past her and go to Adrian, sitting next to him on the couch. I can feel the sets of at least fifty pairs of eyes on us. All the vampires who took fledglings this year are here, as are their humans. Kelly sits on his other side and leans back, appearing disinterested.

"Where's Cameron?" he asks her.

"He's out." Two words and his entire demeanor goes frigid.

"And this is the first I'm hearing of it?"

"Sorry," she mumbles. "I don't know what happened."

"I can tell you what happened," I speak up, "and it's not Kelly's fault." I don't know why I'm helping her when she continues to treat me like trash, but maybe I feel bad for her.

"Is that so?" Adrian turns back to me. "I see you didn't bother to dress for the occasion, nor have you taken care of your little problem, like I asked."

I narrow my eyes. "It's my choice, asshole. It's my body and I decide what goes on it and who touches it."

"Come." He stands, hauling me up. "We need to discuss this in private."

When Kelly stands, he points to her. "You stay here. Keep an eye on things."

There's a little hallway at the back of the room and he leads me into one of the unmarked doors. It's some kind of VIP suite for privacy. I can only imagine what it's usually used for, and my cheeks flame. I don't want to be alone with this guy anymore. I shouldn't even be here.

I turn on him. "You need to be nicer to Kelly." Here I go defending her again when she screwed me over.

"Oh, you mean the woman responsible for your poor choice in outfit tonight?" He motions to me. "Because I can assure you I'm no fool. I know she didn't tell you to dress up."

I shrug. "I like how I look."

"Is that so?"

I square my shoulders. "Yes."

"Very well, though I find it strange you're defending Kelly. Do you realize she's mad that you're my fledgling?"

I narrow my eyes. "Well, tell her it's not really going to happen. That's what you said, right? You'd entertain this game but didn't actually plan to turn me."

He slaps his hand over my mouth and pushes me against the wall, glaring. "Keep your voice down. Do you know how many listening ears are around anytime I'm in public? If that got back to Brisa, you'd be dead."

I push him off. "Fine, but don't touch me."

"What is this about Kelly's fledgling? What do you know?"

"Tell me what you know about Tate," I return. "Why is he messing with people's memories?"

"I suspected this but you just confirmed it for me." He begins to pace the little room. "I knew they could sometimes wipe minds like that, but I didn't think anyone had developed the ability in over a century."

"What are you talking about?"

His eyes land on me. "It's better that you don't know."

"Says you, maybe." I frown. "But am I safe going there? Are my friends safe training underneath Tate?"

"Probably not," he supplies, "but they're humans, so they're not safe anywhere." He comes closer. "And neither are you."

Closer. Closer. Closer. I'm back up against the wall, and he's leaning into me. I think maybe he's going to bite me. My heart rate speeds up, and my mouth waters. I kinda, sorta, maybe ... want him to bite me. It must be the venom. It's reaching out, clearing my mind of any objections.

He runs the cool tip of his nose along my neck and then up to whisper in my ear. "What have you seen him do?"

"Huh?"

He chuckles and pulls back. "What have you seen Tate do? What else do you know of him?"

"He returned last week. Everyone's acting like he never left. Nobody questions him. He brought me into his office and told me to trust him. I did, but part of me fought back, I think because of Hugo's venom." I whisper that last part. "So I followed him to a hospital ICU. He did some kind of energy exchange thing there. Do you know what I'm talking about? Where they steal energy from humans?"

He nods once.

"So, what are they?"

"Like I said, it's better if you don't know."

"You're really annoying."

Someone knocks on the door.

"Come in," Adrian says, albeit a little reluctantly.

I'm expecting it to be Kelly.

It's not.

CHAPTER 11

"I've been looking for you," the man says.

Hugo.

Not Hugo. Hugo is dead.

Hugo is dead.

But this man looks eerily like Hugo. I want to run, to scream, to fight––anything. But I'm frozen to the spot. My senses grow the most they have since I was bit, almost drowning me with smell and sight and ... I can't think. I need to go.

"Sebastian, I didn't expect to see you here," Adrian says. His voice comes at me loud and fast, but also like he's speaking through a wall of glass.

"Brisa is allowing me to investigate my twin's death." The man saunters into the room, his lip curled up like he just smelled something rotten. So that's why I thought it was Hugo. Sebastian looks exactly like the dead vampire––Italian, broad-shouldered, handsome, middle-aged, and creepy. And now he's here to *investigate?*

"That's good," Adrian says smoothly, "I hope you can catch the hunters who did this. I've been looking for them myself but so far have no leads."

Sebastian's eyes flick to mine. "Why do you smell so good?" His fangs begin to extend. Oh, so maybe not rotten.

"Virgin blood." Adrian positions himself in front of me. "She's mine."

I'm his––it's the same thing Kelly said. What have I gotten myself into?

I flash back to how Hugo figured out I was connected into his line. My blood had spilled, and that's all it took. That could happen again. One wrong move and it'll all be over. Being here is more dangerous than ever. I never should've pushed for this. What do I really think I'll learn that can help the hunters? So far all I've done is put myself in danger.

Sebastian's fangs retract, but his pupils stay dilated and his eyes remain on me. "You know, I've always found it frustrating that so much of the archaic vampire lore happens to be true. We can't go in the sun. We're allergic to silver. We're killed with a stake to the heart. We're even adverse to garlic––it smells horrible and I'm Italian. Such a pity."

"And you're born in cemeteries," I add, trying to make my voice sound light.

"We are." His head tilts. "But being attracted to the blood of virgins? That's one I've never minded."

"What's so special about it?" Adrian stiffens when I ask the question.

"Nobody knows," the man smiles, "but it works both ways. Did you know that? We're more attracted to you," he steps forward, "and you're more attracted to us. Back in the day, priests used to have virgins walk through graveyards at night looking for vampire graves. The girls could sometimes spot our newly buried prodigy's graves, and the priests would dig them up and stake them before they had a chance to fully change." His smile turns mocking. "Now, tell me, who's more barbaric?"

I've always hated vampires, but maybe this explains part of why it was easier for me to track that one. I had venom from the same line and virgin blood. Maybe I really am special. I shoot a charged look at Adrian--no wonder he wanted me to "take care of it."

"So what would happen if a fledgling was turned into a prodigy while still a virgin?"

"That's--"

"Let's go," Adrian cuts him off, "we have business to attend to."

I want to object and ask Sebastian to finish but the two are looking at each other now like they hate each other, like their history is even worse than Hugo's, and it's as if I'm no longer in the room.

"Ah, that's right." Sebastian wiggles his fingers. "Pretend I'm a fly on the wall."

As if that were possible.

Adrian takes my hand and squeezes, his way of telling me to stick close. I wonder what the implications of Sebastian being here means for me. Is he going to figure out what happened that night? Will they turn me? Kill me? What will happen to Adrian? If Hugo was a prince, then surely Sebastian is one as well.

When we get back to the main room, it's filled up with more vampires and their fledglings. Standing room only. Adrian sits me next to Kelly, who's now got Cameron at her side. I gape at him. He forgot everything so why is he here? Kelly nods toward him. "He showed up here a couple minutes ago. Apparently it all came back to him and he's on our side."

But how? Is Tate's ability not as strong as I thought?

"Hey," Cameron whispers when he sees me.

"You remembered?"

He nods curtly. "Yup."

I don't have a good feeling about this. Something isn't adding up.

"Get all the humans who aren't prodigies out of this building," Adrian instructs one of his minions who takes off in a flash--literally. These creatures can move so fast that sometimes they look like a flash.

We mingle for a few minutes, but I don't offer much to the conversations. I'm listening intently though, hoping for something I can bring back to Seth. My eyes keep going from Adrian to Sebastian and back again.Sebastian is even more charismatic than his brother was, the creepiness factor not quite there. That's got to make him more dangerous. People flock to him, and he engages a crowd with practiced ease, moving through them like I imagine a prince should. He's a true diplomat.

Adrian seems annoyed. This is his territory, after all. And his coven. But he hides it well, or maybe we're all used to Adrian being annoyed. The dancers have long been sent away by the time Adrian strides to the center of the room and then levitates, hovering above the busy crowd. Everyone falls silent, their leader commanding attention without having to say a word. Several of the humans gaze up at him like he's a god or something. It's hard not to glower at them.

"Thank you for coming," Adrian says. "Many of you already know how this is going to work, but some of you have waited for me to explain it to your humans." His blue gaze seems to glow as he surveys the room, making a point to look at us fledglings. Right now we're nothing, but soon we'll be their prodigies. Maybe. "You are not guaranteed a spot in our coven even though you've been selected to be the next prodigy to your masters. You must prove your loyalty and utility. When your master feels you are ready, he or she will petition the queen. Only Brisa can decide who joins our fold and when."

Damn. I knew Brisa was controlling, but this is next level.

"There is no set rule in our coven about how, when, or where to test you. We do things a little differently each year so that the playing field stays level. Once you are ready, you will be turned. If you are deemed unworthy, however," his voice drops an octave, "well, let's just say you don't want to find out what happens to you then."

They kill us.

He doesn't have to say more, it's apparent. Maybe because we know too much. Probably because they can get away with it. Either way, my mouth grows dry. Nervous whispers ignite throughout the room, spreading to every corner. The fledglings are all young, athletic-looking, beautiful people. Everyone has a chance. And I hate them all. They're here because they want immortality, even at the cost of human lives. If I look hard enough, I can see their auras. The colors are dingy, dark, and not bright and happy like so many other humans I've been able to see. I wish I could see my own aura, but I can't. Would mine be pretty or would mine be dirty? At least I'm only here because I'm a double agent, sent to help the humans.

"Your first test starts now. You will go out into the city and bring back a human to do a willing blood donation within the hour. What we do with that donor is up to us." The vampires laugh as we sit here, letting this challenge sink in. Shouldn't be too hard, right? Except what do I have to offer someone to get them to come back here? It almost sounds like we're supposed to go find someone to sacrifice. "Well, go on." Adrian flicks his wrist. "The clock is ticking."

"Come on," I get up, nodding to Cameron, "are we going to do this or what?"

We go outside, and Cameron veers off without me. I shake my head and shoot a middle finger to his back. "Jerk," I mumble.

I don't want to do this.

I'm not really going to be a prodigy, I hate the fledglings, and I take zero delight in finding someone to become a vampire's snack. What will happen if I go back there empty handed?

I don't know what to do. If it were only Adrian here, I'd refuse this request. But it's not only Adrian here, and there are eyes on him now, eyes reporting back to the queen, eyes looking to avenge their dead twin brother.

And I'm all alone. I'm keenly aware that I'm a young woman alone at night in a very dangerous city. This is not a place I want to be.

I can't do this.

I can't bring someone up there. What if they kill them? Sure, they may only get willing donations, but I've seen vampires kill before. I saw Adrian do it. I later figured out that it was a mobster he'd killed, and maybe someone who deserved it, but Adrian hadn't wanted me to know that. He'd wanted me to believe that it was

98

someone who didn't deserve it. That he was a ruthless killer. He wanted me to see who he really was so that I wouldn't be stupid enough to keep coming around. I should've listened.

That's when the idea strikes me.

CHAPTER 12

I walk across the street to the casino, heading past the tables and right for the nurses' office. "Hey, do you guys know who I am?"

The woman at reception stares at me blankly and shakes her head. I sigh and head for the tables, looking for one of the pit bosses. Sure enough, I find the very same guy who pissed me off the first day I met Adrian. *Well, this is going to be fun.* I motion to him with my finger and to my delight, he comes right away.

"You know who I am, right? You can vouch for me?" I ask.

He groans under his breath but nods.

"Great. Follow me. We have to do something for Adrian."

I turn and stride back to the nurses' station. I don't bother to see if he followed because I can sense him at my back.

"Me again," I say to the same lady from before. "He can vouch for me. I work for Adrian."

She raises an eyebrow and the vampire answers. "Adrian instructed us to keep her safe and do whatever she needs." With that, he shoots me a glare and then turns and walks away.

I don't care. I've perked up at his confession, warmth spreading through me. More news and this time it's actually good news.

"Right." I smile back at the woman. "Adrian says I'm supposed to bring one of you across the street to do blood donations over there at the club."

The lady frowns. "Are they short-staffed again?"

Okay, I can work with this. "Oh, you know how it is. There's always another human in line. Can I walk someone over?"

"Hold on," she says, "I'll grab a nurse for you."

Five minutes later, I'm walking back across the street with Nurse Giggi at my side, hoping this isn't a huge mistake. My nerves are like a coil of angry snakes raging in my belly, but I can't think about that right now. Technically, this is what Adrian asked for, and he should know I have a way with twisting his words.

When we get back to the nightclub VIP area, we're one of the first to arrive. Adrian is sitting with Sebastian, their heads bent together in deep conversation. Nothing about Adrian's demeanor exposes his guilt. He's had how many years now to perfect his lying capabilities? I need to remember that next time I want to believe him about something.

"Here you go," I say, interrupting them. "The human you asked for."

They stop and stare up at me. Adrian's mouth thins. "Who's this?"

"You told us to bring you a human for blood donations." Poor Nurse Giggi stiffens at my side as I continue. "Well, that's what she is, right? She's trained in taking donations."

The room is quiet, the waiting vampires watching our exchange, when Sebastian bursts into laughter. His energy is so different than Hugo's had been, so open and charismatic. I can't imagine Hugo ever had a sense of humor. Adrian doesn't have much of one either, because his mouth is still thinned and his eyes are glued to me.

"Do you not need my services?" Giggi balks and steps back.

Adrian holds up a hand to stop her. "Actually, I think you should stay. We can always use more help." He nods over to the corner of the room and tells her to wait over there.

"Your lady is something else." Sebastian gives me a wink. "You sure you want to be with this guy? I could get you into my bloodline during my next prodigy cycle."

Hmm, I've heard that one before.

"Very funny." Adrian grabs me, pulling me down to sit in his lap. My heart rate speeds up, and he leans down to whisper against my cheek. "You like to push my buttons, don't you?"

I elbow him in the chest, which does nothing but hurt my funny bone. I try not to wince but I do and he chuckles darkly. "You make it so easy. How is that my fault?"

He tightens his grip around my stomach but doesn't say anything more. I could move. I could slide to his side or get up––anything––and I'm certain he'd let me. But I don't. We have to appear like we want this to work. I'm more than a little grateful he didn't kill me for skirting around his dumb assignment. I'm not sure I'll be able to keep doing that.

"You're quite clever," Sebastian says, turning on me with his dark gaze. "Tell me, did you have the opportunity to meet my brother?"

I nod.

"Right answer," he says. He must already know. Adrian said he was going to tell Brisa that I was there that night. I try to get the story straight in my mind, but it goes annoyingly blank. "Lying to a vampire is a terrible idea."

I'm not going to let this guy get the best of me.

"I don't have a death wish. Well, that's unless it comes with a three night stay in a graveyard." I wink playfully. "So ask me anything. I was there that night Hugo was killed by those hunters. I have nothing to hide."

"So forthright," Sebastian says. "Okay, how did it happen? I want every detail."

"Now is not really the time," Adrian says, "we can schedule an appointment for this if you'd like."

"Now is the perfect time." I elbow Adrian again. "Like I said, there's nothing to hide. I was supposed to be Adrian's fledgling, but Hugo took over and was going to be my master instead. They took me to the graveyard together, but hunters showed up, killing your brother before we could do anything. Adrian saved me and then stepped in to be my master once again. And that's about it, Sebastian. I'm sorry about your twin. We tried to help, but we were ambushed."

"Hmm," Sebastian says, "I can see why you picked her, Adrian."

"I didn't pick her," Adrian replies, "she picked me."

"Well isn't that adorable."

"You know what I mean. I don't believe in building our family lines. We're more vulnerable when there's too many of us. We're too open to mistakes, especially our younger spawn. But it was time to add another to my line and this one asked for the role."

The two men stare off like they're either about to debate with words or with fists.

"Whatever." I slip off Adrian's lap and sit at the end of the couch. I'm not getting between those two. "I'm a woman who makes her own choices, and I wanted to become a vampire. What's so wrong with that?"

"And as a woman who makes her own choices,"

Sebastian's tone shifts, turning slightly accusatory as he glares at me, "why would you choose to become a vampire? You'll be beholden to Adrian, and through Adrian to Brisa, for the rest of your existence."

That's if they don't die first. But I don't add that thought. "Because I'd rather be immortal. I want to be able to feel and experience the world to its fullest, like you can."

"That's a clichéanswer." He gets up and comes to stand above me, leaning in close. His pupils dilate, and his fangs peek through his lips. "What's the truth?"

I dig deep, searching for a better answer. The truth? I hate vampires. I want them eradicated from the planet. But why? So I can feel safe. So I can live without looking over my shoulder. So I can have all the things I deserved to have that were stolen from me when my mother became an addict.

"Tell me," he demands, inching closer.

Adrian holds him back. "Leave her."

"Because I want to feel safe," I grind out. "Because I want to be taken care of. Because I want a real family."

Both men relax. Pity creeps into Adrian's eyes, and I have to look away.

Sebastian points at me as he steps away. "The truth will set you free."

Okay, lame. Who does this guy think he is? Jerry Maguire?

"That's enough," Adrian says. "We need to move this along." He motions to the room, which has filled up with people. They're mingling among each other, the humans easy to pick out in the crowd. Some seem nervous, their eyes darting from sucker to sucker, and some seem excited. Cameron is there, a young woman in club attire at his side. They chat casually, but his body language is stiff and uncertain.

The vampires stand and circle the humans, their eyes growing hungry. This might not be what I thought it was. What if this is a bloodbath? What if they kill all these humans and dispose of the bodies discreetly? There's got to be at least twenty humans who aren't fledglings. Surely they can't cover up twenty deaths. The Vampire Enforcement Coalition wouldn't allow it.

Or would they?

I'm starting to suspect the VEC is nothing but a farce and a way for them to pretend like they're behaving, and another way to assert power over each other––big egos versus even bigger egos. Because if a human gets bit, they're as good as dead. Vampires don't want humans to have the senses that I have and I can see why, now that it's burning through me. It would make us all excellent fighters, able to track them, able to kill them easier. What if every human in the world was able to get the venom injected into them, kind of like a vaccine? We'd become strong enough to fight them, maybe even end them all.

If I could somehow get the word out, somehow find a way . . .

"Well done," Adrian says, "now let's eat."

I expect the vampires to pounce, for blood to fly and bodies to hit the floor.

Nurses appear with all the necessary supplies and begin taking blood. They even have little handheld devices to see who's eligible to give and how much. The entire thing is completely legal and anticlimactic. Nurse Giggi is among them and she gives me a little wave when we make eye contact.

I don't think I've ever been more grateful for an anticlimactic moment.

This was a test. Would we risk another's life for the vampires? We passed, but I don't feel any better than I did before.

Just as I start to relax, start to think that everyone is going to get out of here alive, everything changes. Cameron dives on Kelly with a guttural scream, a silver stake firm in his hand. It sinks right through her center. She screams.

CHAPTER 13

*K*elly evaporates into dust.

I scream.

It's not like those other times I saw vampires die. There's no joy in this. I feel her loss immediately, like the stake went through my own heart. Kelly wasn't a friend, per se, but I liked her and thought maybe . . .

I don't know what I thought.

But she's gone, and my senses burst to life once again. Cameron stands against the railing, stakes in both hands, ready to fight. He sneers, looking right at me. "That vile sucker showed up last night and insisted that I was hers and told me to come here. And so I do and here you are––"

He never finishes his sentence. Adrian flies at him, ripping the stakes from his hands as if they're children's toys. He tosses them to the ground with a clatter.

Cameron opens his arms wide, accepting his fate.

But his eyes are frantic––death isn't what he wants. It's too late. Adrian pushes Cameron over the railing. Cameron doesn't even scream on his way down. He disappears from view, followed by a quick dull thump. Adrian growls savagely and jumps down after him.

Sebastian follows.

As do several others.

I stand frozen, unwilling to look over the railing and see for myself. A few of the humans run over to watch, while most of us crowd to the back of the room. We can all hear what's happening. Personally, I don't need to see it, too.

A couple minutes later, Adrian flies up, hovering midair. His appearance causes a ripple of gasps from almost everyone in the room. Not me. His eyes are bloodshot. I didn't know that happened to vampires. Does it have something to do with anger rather than bloodlust? Or maybe it's because he just fed from human flesh, not a blood bag. Whatever it is, the sight sends a chill right through me. Blood drips from his mouth and stains the top of his crisp white shirt.

"Go home." His voice is eerily calm, but I can trace the grief there. Kelly was his only prodigy, and now she's nothing but dust. "Go home and tell everyone what you saw here. Tell them how a hunter tried to take us out when we were obeying the law. We did nothing wrong. He murdered one of our own in cold blood and would've killed more if he had the chance. Tell them exactly what happened." His eyes land on me. "And let them know we will root out anyone who hurts us. And when we do, we will kill them. No hunter in this city is safe."

He zooms away, practically disappearing into thin air.

I leave with everyone else, guilt wracking me as I do. I want to go to Adrian and explain what I think happened here, to make sure he doesn't blame me. But maybe he should blame me. I failed to protect Kelly, didn't I? I should've known this could happen. The moment I saw Cameron in here, I should've stopped him. In his mind, all he knew was that vampires were bad and he should kill them. Tate made him forget the rest. So Kelly showing up and telling him he's her fledgling last night must have freaked him out. But he did come, and then he acted on his training. And now they're both dead.

And here you are . . .

What was he going to say? Was he going to reveal who I am to everyone? Was he expecting me to help him? I'll never know. Maybe it's better that I don't.

I go to the casino. I want to head up to Adrian's office so we can talk about this but the elevator won't open. I try the penthouse elevator, which does work, and I head up to his room instead. I knock on the door, but he doesn't answer. I'm sure he's probably in there, but he won't come to the door. I don't have his number either. My only contact is calling The Alabaster when I need to relay a message through Kelly. I'm not sure what to do now.

"Listen," I call through the door, "I'm sorry about what happened. Do you have my number?" He doesn't reply and maybe I'm talking to thin air. I tell him the number anyway, assuming he can memorize it. And then I leave.

When I locate my Porsche in the parking garage, Sebastian appears next to me; I nearly jump out of my skin.

"Geez! Do you have manners? You shouldn't sneak up on someone like that." My heart beats wildly and my senses grow.

"It comes with the territory." That's true. I don't think vampires know how to be loud.

I fold my arms over my chest. "How can I help you, Sebastian?"

"You can explain what happened back there."

None of your business.

We stop and stare off. This is the part where I lie and tell him I have no idea. But I don't. I know I can't be compelled, and I know I can't trust this guy, but something inside of me spills the truth.

"I'm a hunter, too. Adrian knows." I hold up my hands before he rips my head off. "I'm working for Adrian. How do you think I got the guy who insists he doesn't want a family line to agree to take me on as his fledgling?"

Sebastian looks me up and down. "If you're lying, I will find out, and I will kill you."

I laugh. "Believe me, I know."

"So is this how my brother died?"

"No, he died as we said he did. Hunters ambushed us and killed him."

He studies me for a long while. "You know, someone is going around and killing off the princes. Brisa has lost almost all her direct prodigies, Hugo included. It's my job to find out who's doing it and deliver them to her."

My mouth falls open a little. "I've not heard anything about this."

"There will be dire consequences for the humans if the bloodlines are severed," he goes on. "Brisa is the best thing that's ever happened to humankind."

It takes everything in me not to snort because this guy has got to be delusional. She's the reason vampires are out in public, the mastermind behind this system of trading blood for addictions. I hate her with everything in me. Killing her would be my dream come true. "And how do you figure that?"

"Because without her, our one strong vampire bloodline would splinter off into several independent lines. Do you know how many vampires would love nothing more than to feed and kill whoever they wanted? And they would be free to do that because nobody would be able to tell them not to."

I have no response to that and feel stupid that I'd never thought of it. But it makes sense, and it flips my entire world upside down. I should get out of this. Return the fancy car, refuse to be a fledgling anymore, drop the hunters, everything. Just be done.

I should, but I won't. I'm not sure I even can at this point.

"Adrian is going to be grieving his child," Sebastian continues, his voice growing cold. "So it's a good thing he has you to tend to his broken heart. Can you imagine how he'd feel if you had died tonight as well? If someone wanted to get back at him, say someone who lost his twin recently for no good reason, well, I think your death would be the perfect move."

I widen my stance, my mind racing to the thin stake under my shirt. Could I get to it in time?

"But don't worry," Sebastian continues, "I'd never do such a thing to my own brother." He strolls off, whistling as he does, as if he didn't just threaten my life to get back at Adrian. He rounds the corner, disappearing, but his nasally tune echoes through the parking garage for another full minute.

I don't hear from Adrian. September crawls into October, and life continues as if I weren't a vampire's fledgling at all. Felix and I go back to being friends without benefits, even though it's hard. So many times I catch him staring at me in a way that sends my heart fluttering. I want to kiss him––to do more than kiss him––but I don't. Things have gotten too complicated. Between his past with my roommate, Ayla refusing to talk to me, Seth telling me to back off, and mostly because I'm not a very safe person to date right now, it's better that I go back to waiting.

Waiting for Felix is something I'm used to, even though it's killing me.

I keep expecting the venom to wear off, but it doesn't. I've quickly become the top member on my team, able to fight faster than anyone else. Even the simulations are easy for me now. And the more I grow in my abilities, the more I can sense things I never could before. And the more I can see things. But I know the simulations aren't the real thing, and I'm eager to hunt.

Too bad I'm in an impossible situation. Being a double agent sucks.

One day, I'm driving back from a dayshift at Pops, marveling at the swirls of colors surrounding all the people as they walk down the sidewalks. It's crowded today, and the auras remind me of misty clouds bouncing into each other. There's roadwork on my usual route, so I follow the GPS down a curvy side street. It's narrow with tall buildings that cast cool shadows down below. There are shops here I haven't seen before, so I drive a little slow and look at the pretty storefronts. There's an eclectic gift shop, a clothing boutique, an independent bookstore, a little bakery, and a voodoo shop.

A lot of the businesses down in this part of town say they deal in voodoo as a way to bring tourists in. I don't know how much of it is authentic, but either way, it's something I've chosen to stay away from. Growing up in New Orleans, a lot of the parents and grandparents teach their kids that voodoo is dangerous. I'm not sure what parts of voodoo are considered a closed-practice and what aren't, what's safe or even real. I'm not going to judge anyone who practices religion, but it's not my thing. Never has been. Never will be.

Never say never, right?

Because something catches my eye, a bright flash of golden reflective light in my peripheral vision. The window display of the voodoo shop is filled to the brim with little dolls and trinkets, nothing unusual. Except there's also a golden metal decoration. It's two crossing feathers in the same shape as the little stamp on the back of the silver cross I wear around my neck. It seems far-fetched, especially since a cross is typically a Christian symbol, but maybe my grandmother bought the neck-lace there.

The same grandmother who made me promise to stay away from voodoo. So why do I have the feeling she was hiding something?

I parallel park like a pro. It was the one thing I spent hours practicing for the driver's exam and aced with flying colors, which is important living in a busy city. I climb out of the car and head into the shop before my sweet gran's voice in my head can stop me. The bell chimes as I enter, but nobody comes to check on me. It doesn't seem like anyone's even in here. The shop is tiny and packed. Skull candles, jewelry, herbs, crystals, loads more of the dolls, and a bunch of other things that I'm not sure how to identify. I go to the window display and crane my neck to try to get a better look at the golden feathers.

Just as I thought, it's an exact match for the one stamped on the back of my cross. Upon first inspection, it looks like any other simple design of feathers and nothing too special, but there's a little hook at the bottom of the left feather that makes it distinctive.

Mine has the same one. I pinch it between my fingers and an eerie sense of foreboding prickles down my body.

"Can I help you?" a scratchy voice croons.

I turn to find a tiny middle-aged woman with creamy tanned skin and long braided hair staring at me. She's beautiful but immediately I can sense her anger. It reminds me of Kelly and my heart drops.

"I was wondering if you could tell me about these feathers?" I ask politely.

She glares at me, which is certainly an odd way to treat a customer. "What do you want with that talisman, girl?"

My mouth pops open, but I recover quickly, folding my arms over my chest. My politeness was short-lived. "Listen, I don't know what your problem is with me, but I'm a potential customer and––"

"No, you're not." She shoos me to the door. "Get out of here."

I gape at her. I've never had such a strange interaction with a salesperson, and it's obvious the woman is trying to get me out of here before I can learn what that talisman is for. I've watched enough CW shows to know a talisman is an object that holds a spell.

I pull the cross out from under the neckline of my shirt and flip it over, showing her the little stamp. "My grandmother gave this to me. She wore it her whole life as far as I know. Her and my mom have insisted I wear it now, too."

"A lot of people wear crucifixes to ward off vampires, which is silly because it doesn't work."

"I want to know about the feathers. My gran is dead or I'd ask her myself."

"What does this have to do with me?" The woman stomps past me and opens the door. "You need to leave or I'll call the police."

"No, look," I press, "on the back of it, see? There's a little feather. It's the same one."

The woman stares at me for a long moment, her eyes going from my face to the necklace and back again. Her demeanor stays hard. "It's for protection," she barks out.

"The feather or the cross?"

I already know the cross is supposed to be protection, but Adrian had no issue ripping it from my throat. It didn't do anything to hurt him, but maybe that's because the chain wasn't real silver. Maybe it was, I'm not sure, but it easily could've been something else. I definitely think the new chain is silver though, Felix wouldn't mess around or lie to me about that.

"Superstitions run deep around here," she says. "Both."

My eyes start to water. "My grandmother was my favorite person in the whole wide world." Losing her nearly killed me and Mom.

"I'm sorry for your loss," she grinds out. "Keep wearing the feathers."

So really, it's the feathers that mattered to gran, not the cross like she led me to believe.

"Protection from what?"

She swallows and then whispers. "Listen, I don't want anything to do with this. You shouldn't have come here."

"Are you talking about vampires?" I whisper. "Or something else?"

She stills. That's it then. Does this symbol have something to do with the energy demon things? Is this protection from them? I always thought it was for the vampires, but maybe I was wrong. I wonder how much my gran knew. I wonder what would happen if I showed it to Tate. Would he freak out? Would he be fine?

"Please . . ." My voice cracks. "I have nowhere else to go."

"You don't have a place here either, and trust me, you do not want to get on my bad side," she hisses. She points to one of the dolls, which I know are used for hexes, and that's when I decide maybe I'd better listen. I can't even leave a bad review online for fear of retribution. I never thought I believed in any of this stuff, but turns out I sorta do.

I go back to my car and stare at the window display for a few minutes. How could a question about a feather symbol cause such an upset? The answer is because they mean something important, something to do with protection that she doesn't want to discuss with me. I wince, realizing that the more I look for answers, the more questions I end up with. Hours roll by and I'm still thinking about the necklace.

CHAPTER 14

I knock on the Morenos' door, and a few minutes later Mrs. Moreno opens it. "Eva, it's so good to see you honey." She hugs me, but she comes out onto the doorstep to do it. It's the first time she doesn't immediately invite me inside.

"Is Ayla here?" I ask tentatively.

The woman steps back and frowns. "I'm sorry, she's not seeing guests right now."

I blink at her, unsure how to respond. Ayla has been my bestie for ages and I still can't believe this is happening. "Nobody?"

Mrs. Moreno shakes her head with a little frown. "We're trying to respect her wishes," her voice cracks and she whispers. "We don't know what to do. She's refusing to leave the house. The therapist says it's an anxiety disorder called agoraphobia."

"But she won't let anyone visit her either?"

Her eyes water. "Not even Felix. She won't talk to anyone. We don't know what to do. At this point, our main concern is keeping her alive." She wipes a tear. "I never thought this would happen to one of our kids."

I wring my hands behind my back, my emotions torn to shreds. I should probably tell her about the vampire attack, but that would involve revealing Felix's secrets. And I'm pretty sure Ayla would be upset if I did, but my friend's safety and happiness is important. I want her to heal. Ayla's made of tough stuff, always has been, so to see her like this is terrible.

In the end, I decide to go half way. "Is the therapist doing house calls?"

"They're doing video conferencing. Ayla gets upset at the thought of anyone coming into the house."

Yeah, because she's afraid of vampires, and vampires have to be invited into a private residence. It makes sense. It doesn't make sense that she's turning humans away, but her mind is probably having a hard time separating it all.

"You should tell the therapist to talk to Ayla about a possible fear of vampires."

Mrs. Moreno's face goes pale and she does the sign of the cross, muttering to herself in Spanish. "Has Ayla seen a vampire?"

"I have to go," I say, backing away. "But trust me, there's something there."

I go back and sit in the car for a while. Then I get out and go to the side of the house where I can knock on

Ayla's window. The curtains are drawn, so I can't see in, but I know she's got to be in there. I pull out my phone and text her.

Are you okay? We should talk.

I told you not to come back here, is her immediate reply. She knows I'm out here which is probably why she replied to me at all.

I have something to tell you. Please, at least come to the window.

A minute later the curtain moves and Ayla cracks the window. Not enough for me to go in or anything, but enough so we can talk. I jog over and study her through the reflective glass. Her hair is in a messy bun on the top of her head, her eyes are sunken, and she's wearing oversized pajamas.

"Hey," I keep my voice low and smooth. "Are you okay?"

"What did you want to tell me?" She folds her arms over her chest and lifts a messy eyebrow. It's another reminder of how much my friend has changed. She's hurting, sick, and I want to help her. I wish I knew how to rewind everything.

"I broke it off with Felix, but that's not all I wanted to say."

"Trouble in paradise? I could've told you he's a player." Her voice is annoyed.

"I broke it off because I don't think it's the best idea right now."

"Oh, right now, huh? So you're still going to hook up with my brother later on?"

I sigh heavily and grind my sandal into the grass. "Ugh, I don't know, Ayla, that's not what this is about."

"Okay, fine, what else is so important that you had to disrespect my wishes by coming and knocking on my window? You already know how I feel. I don't want you hunting, and you're hunting. I don't want you dating my brother, and you did it behind my back. What else is there to talk about?"

My eyes water. "You're my best friend."

"Not anymore."

"What?" My voice cracks.

"Because I've changed." Her eyes narrow. "People change and grow up and move on. You need to get over it."

Despite everything I've gone through with my mom, this is the worst betrayal I've ever experienced. My heart squeezes, and the hot tears finally release, running down my cheeks. "I was going to say sorry and that I am here for you. I wanted to show you my apartment. I wanted--"

"Just go home." Her voice is regretful. "I wish things were different, okay? But as long as you're involved with hunting vampires, I can't be your friend."

"So you're asking me to choose?"

"You already did." And then she slams the window shut, the curtains sliding back into place. My heart shuts down equally hard.

I never thought this would happen. I completely took our friendship for granted. But I'm angry, too. Because this is Ayla's choice, and she's not even going to try. One scary experience with vampires and that's it, she's shut out anyone and anything she can that could possibly put her in danger again. I don't blame her, but this extreme isn't healthy. She's locked herself in her room during the days now too. Vampires can't go out in sunlight, so what does she think is going to happen?

And yet . . . my gut says something is off––that there's more to the story. I want to help her fix the ending, but she won't let me.

"Nobody knows what happened to Cameron?" Tate asks. We look around at each other, but nobody speaks up.

He's called us in for an emergency meeting because it's been so long since Cameron has disappeared. There isn't room for everyone in his office, so we're sitting on the gym mats in our teams. Each team consists of three to five people who were recruited together. We're all young enough that our prefrontal cortexes haven't fully developed, ranging in age from eighteen to twenty-four, and Cameron was getting near that cut off. Soon Tate would've been wiping his mind clear of any memories of his time with the hunters, except that's impossible now that he's dead.

I look around, really hoping that we're all humans

here. I blink a few times, concentrating, and the auras start to materialize. As far as I can tell, everyone has one. Everyone except for Leslie Tate, that is.

Someone in the back raises his hand. "I think I might know something," he says with a regretful tone.

My heart riots against my ribcage, adrenaline racing through my limbs. I'm frozen, my breath trapped in my lungs. I feel as if everyone is staring at me, but I know they're not. I wish I could debrief my team on everything that's happened, but I don't trust Tate anymore and they're too close to him. What if he was able to get information out of them that I didn't want him to know? I hate that Cameron's death is something I've had to keep to myself.

"What do you know, Kevin?" Tate walks toward the guy, and once he passes us, I relax a little. I exchange worried glances with my team. Kenton reaches over to squeeze my hand. It's completely platonic, we've become great friends, and I'm struck by how grateful I am for him. Nobody will ever replace Ayla, but it's nice to know I have a friend like Kenton in my corner.

"I've only heard rumors." Kevin stands up and addresses the room. "But apparently a hunter tried to attack vampires during one of their meetups. He killed one of them." He swallows hard. "That's the good news."

"And the bad news?"

He doesn't have to say it—everybody knows—but he does anyway. "They ripped him to pieces. By the time they were done with him, there wasn't anything left."

We're all quiet. Nobody's surprised. It's part of the risks in doing what we're doing, and nobody is stupid enough to come here thinking they'll be the exception. We hope we'll survive and assume we won't. It's the life of a vampire hunter.

"Thank you," Tate says. He turns back to all of us. "This is why we do what we do. We have to defeat these monsters."

But how? Honestly, how are we going to end them? They're all over the planet. They're everywhere. And they can turn more of us into them anytime they want. Sometimes this mission seems helpless.

"We're going to take back our city," Tate says, "we've been too soft, too slow, and too careful."

Careful? Cameron is dead, and Tate's telling us we're being too careful.

"It's time we get them in one swoop," Tate continues. "There's a meetup tomorrow at the Alabaster Heart with the entire coven. Every vampire in New Orleans will be there."

His gaze locks us in. "And we're going to pay them a visit. It's time to end this coven and take back our city. Are you in?"

It's a death wish. We can't do this. We may be able to get some of them, but there's no way we could get them all. And even if we did, the vampires from other cities would retaliate.

There's no way to win.

"Our target is Adrianos Teresi. I'll be emailing you all

a breakdown on him. He's the heart of the operation. We take him out first."

Everyone stands up, and I follow. What else can I do? But my legs are shaking and Adrian's face fills my mind.

"Who's in?"

We cheer our agreement, but I know how foolish this is. We're going to end up like Cameron, every last one of us.

CHAPTER 15

"We can't go through with this," I announce the second we're back to Seth and Felix's place. "It's going to be a bloodbath."

"It'd better be!" Kenton laughs. "This is what we've been waiting for. This is our chance."

"I hardly think a few months of training is enough," I scoff. I plop down on the couch and press my palms into my eyes, trying to think. "What benefit would Tate have to take Adrian out?"

"This isn't just about your little vampire prince," Felix interjects. It's the first time he's spoken to me directly since we broke up, not that we were really together for long. But he's avoided me and it's been awful. "Tate wants to clean up New Orleans."

I shake my head. "This has more to do with the vampire royalty than it does our city." I stand and begin to pace the little room. "Vampire princes have been turning up dead all over the world the last few weeks."

"Good," Felix mutters.

Are they even listening to me? "No, not good," I retort. "It's not what you think. If the royals fall, the vamp hierarchy collapses. And that means anarchy."

"What are you saying?" Seth speaks up.

"I am saying that vampires will go back to killing humans for meals. They only follow all these rules about biting and feeding and making their children because the bloodlines are so strong and the queen makes the rules. If the princes die off and the queen is killed, everything they've created will fall apart and not in a good way."

Everyone goes quiet for a while. "And why would Tate want anarchy?" Felix asks.

"I don't know yet." I swallow hard. I don't want to say too much but I have to say enough to get them to understand. "And I know you guys trust him, but I promise you, that feeling is part of his abilities. We all know he's not human, but has he ever told any of you what he is? Have you even asked?"

They stare at me blankly, their faces too relaxed. This is exactly the problem. Tate is powerful enough to get people to believe whatever he says. They know he's different, but they don't question him because he tells them not to. It's only because of Hugo's venom that I'm lucky enough to see through the lies. I never thought I would be grateful for that creepy vampire trying to turn me, but here we are.

"This is getting dangerous," Felix says at last. "Maybe you should stay away."

"Me? How about all of us?"

"No, you."

"Oh, not this again. We already established that I'm part of this team."

"Last I checked you're probably invited to that coven meeting?"

I bite my lip and try not to scream. He's missing the point, trying to make this about something that it's not. "I honestly don't know yet."

"I think Felix has a point," Kenton interjects. "I'm sorry, Eva, but think about it. What if the vampires catch you with us or vice versa? You could end up killed."

I lean forward. "So what do you want me to do? Should I tell Adrian I'm out?"

"No," Seth's voice of reason cuts in, "I think you should be careful about being seen with hunters in public and skip the raid tomorrow. There's got to be something you can learn from that sucker—something that can help us."

I throw my hands up in the air. There shouldn't be a raid tomorrow, but I'm talking in circles with these guys. It's not their fault they're so influenced by Tate, but I'm not about to let my closest friends, the only friends I have left, walk into that casino tomorrow to be slaughtered. So I get up to leave.

"Please, don't go tomorrow. I promise, you won't win. You will die and I can't lose you."

Nobody moves. I leave before they can see me cry. I hate crying. I'm not a crier, damn it.

Felix catches me by my car. He gives the car a frown but I get a sweet smile. "Why are you running off so fast?"

I don't want to explain this to him, there's no point. And the last thing I need is for any of this to get back to Tate. "I've got stuff to do," is all I say.

He steps closer, his warm scent surrounding me. "Are you sure you have to leave?"

"Don't you have to get to class?"

"Not for another hour," he says. "Maybe we could hang out? Talk about things?"

He hasn't brought up the breakup since that first day, but it all comes flooding back now. Most of all, I'm overcome by the feelings I've had for him for so many years. They're so layered that I have a hard time sorting through them. Which ones are old? Which ones are new? Which ones are real?

"I don't want to hurt Ayla," I blurt out.

"Ayla is going through some tough stuff," he says, "and you and I both know it doesn't really have anything to do with us."

I don't know if that's true, but I desperately want to believe it. He leans in closer, trapping me against the car. I like it. A thrill of electricity races up my spine. "And what about the danger? What about the risks?" I whisper.

"We're already putting our lives on the line," he leans in, whispering against my ear, "shouldn't we be allowed to have some fun?"

I don't know if I've ever prioritized fun in my entire life. But I do deserve to have fun. I also need to get rid of my virginity so the vampires stop pestering me about it. Kelly's words float through my head again, and then I remember she's dead, that Cameron's dead, that any of us could go at any time.

Life is short--kiss the boy.

And so I do.

His body presses against mine, his arms wrapping around me, his mouth warm and soft. We kiss for a while, the tension between us growing. For once, I let myself have exactly what I want. I hope Ayla will forgive me and that this choice won't put anyone in danger, but it feels right, and I haven't felt right about anything in so, so long.

This is it.

When we break for a second, I whisper against his soft lips. "Take me upstairs." There's a huskiness to my voice and no doubts about my intentions.

"Are you sure?" he asks.

"Yes."

He peels us apart. "I may sound like I'm an asshole, but I'm trying not to be one for once," he says sheepishly, and I think he's rejecting me. "But I think we should take a little bit of time. I want you to be sure."

Oh.

My cheeks burn. "I said I was sure. I know how I feel."

"But you've had weeks of indecision about us." He wraps me back into a hug and kisses me on the top of the head. "Trust me, this is what I want too. Why don't we meet later tonight after you've had a little more time to think about it? Are you working?"

I shake my head. I guess a few hours isn't the worst thing. "It's my night off."

"Great, tomorrow night we will take down a coven. And tonight, that's for you and me. I promise, okay?"

I'm equal parts annoyed and excited--but I am sure about him, I really am. A couple hours, a couple days, months, or even years won't change my mind about this man. Even if Felix and I don't work out in the end, he's the guy I've been waiting for and the one I want to be my first. I'm not going to let this go. "I'll be back tonight then."

Famous last words . . .

CHAPTER 16

he best way to save my friends is to stop this coven meeting from happening. If they show up to ambush the vampires and there's nobody there to fight with, then hopefully they can walk out of there alive. I may be making a horrible mistake, but once again, I find myself going to Adrian's casino uninvited. When I walk from the sunny outside world and through the double vestibules, the energy shifts. It's opulent inside the casino lobby and I'm used to that. But I'm not used to seeing someone else behind Kelly's desk.

I walk up to the young man and offer a winning smile. "I'm here to meet with Adrian. I'm Evangeline Blackwood." The young man stares at me with a blank expression. He's a vampire alright, and thoroughly creepy. His blond hair is slicked back, and his eyes assess me with dark intentions.

"You don't have an appointment," he says coolly.

"I don't need one," I respond, "I'm his fledgling."

He scoffs. "Honey, all of us were fledglings once upon a time. You think that makes you special? I have news, it doesn't."

I fold my arms over my chest and glare. "Maybe that was your experience, but Adrian treats his fledglings much differently. Do I need to show you my brand new Porsche?"

That was probably the wrong choice of words because the guy's face turns sour. "If you don't have an appointment, then you don't get to demand one without notice. I can fit you in next week, assuming Adrian agrees to take it."

I tap my foot on the tile, growing impatient. "I can't wait until next week."

"That's not my problem."

I grumble and sit down on one of the couches, my eyes trained on the elevator bay. He has to come down eventually, right? Well, that's assuming he's even up there. Hanging out in a vampire's den is not the best idea I've had in a while, but I'm not sure what else to do. So I wait and wait and wait, and the afternoon fades into evening. I'm supposed to go to Felix's place soon, and I need to go home and shower first. But that date seems so unimportant compared to this. I've got to get the vampires to call off their coven meeting tomorrow.

What if I'm making a mistake? What if Adrian uses this information against the hunters? Would he do that? Asked this question a month ago and I would've said yes without a moment's hesitation. But the same question now, and I don't think so. He's not interested in killing the hunters if he can't get to Tate.

And Tate's little plan?

He wants us to kill Adrian without his help. As per the little email that went out, Tate's not even planning to come tomorrow night. So essentially, he's sending the hunters in as sacrificial lambs. I don't know if he cares about our lives, but I kind of doubt it.

Screw this.

I rummage through my wallet, finding the metal key, and smirk. I shoot the executive assistant a dirty glare as I head for the elevators. Assuming he hasn't changed the locks, I still have what I need to get myself into Adrian's penthouse. The ride isn't solo. A human woman gets in with me. She's wearing the tiniest dress I've ever seen. The fabric is a little sheer and I can see her black undergarments.

"Oh, hey," her eyes narrow on me, "aren't you Adrian's fledgling?"

"Yup. I'm Eva."

She extends her hand firmly, and I shake it. "I'm Fiona. I'm Sebastian's fledgling this year. I travel with him wherever he goes."

"Very cool."

Though I don't think it's cool, and the more time I spend around these types of humans, the less I like or understand them. They're not doing this because they think it's right or because they want to help anyone.

They're doing it because they have a sick fascination with vampires and want power. Maybe they want to feel safe, too, but even that is no excuse for signing up and jumping through hoops to impress these suckers.

We make it to the top floor. She goes to the door on the right, and I go left; Sebastian must have taken over Hugo's penthouse. He's a prince, it makes sense. I don't know what to think of Sebastian. Hugo was obviously creepy. Sebastian has charisma for days, but he's kind of like a slimy politician. She knocks softly, and I find it interesting that she doesn't have a key.

When I slide my key into Adrian's lock and turn it easily, I give her a parting goodbye. She doesn't say anything at first, but she does give me a curious look. "You know," she adds, her voice low. "It's weird that Adrian doesn't have a prodigy anymore. Kelly was his only one for years. It's good he has you. People talk."

I scrunch my face up at her, as if anything about that is okay. Like Adrian is so bad because he doesn't turn a human into a monster every chance he can get.

"Let them talk," Adrian's voice cuts sharply from the crack in the door.

The woman freezes.

Adrian snatches me from the hallway, tugging me into the penthouse so fast that my head spins. He slams the door and presses me back against it. "You shouldn't have come here," he hisses.

It's dark inside the room. The shades are drawn over the thick UV-proof windows, and the lights are all off. I can barely see the whites of his eyes, but his presence surrounds me––commanding me to take notice.

"And why's that?"

"Because I'm hungry," he growls under his breath.

"Then eat something." I know he keeps blood stocked in his fridge, and he lives above a blood bank. It's not like he's without food.

He disappears.

Okay, not really, but he flies away so fast that I can't see him do it at all. Then he's in his room, shutting the door and shutting me out. So is this how grief looks in vampires? Shouldn't they be used to death by now? But Kelly was his only "child," and now she's dead. I can't judge him for locking himself in his penthouse, assuming that's what he's doing here.

"That new guy you have sitting in Kelly's desk down there is a real prick," I call out.

"Good," his voice is muffled through the door, "I told him to field all my calls for a few weeks while I grieve."

I don't know why I'm surprised, but I am. I guess I expected Adrian to carry on like business as usual. He's always so in control, so dark and stoic and impenetrable. I never expected him to grieve as humans do, or to call it that. He seems so cold, like nothing could hurt him. Do vampires have therapists?

I flip on the lights.

The place is clean, but it's stuffy as hell. So I turn up the air conditioner since I can't crack a window. Then I rummage through the kitchen drawers until I find some air freshener and spray it around. I go to the fridge where rows of blood bags are stacked inside and plop one in the microwave. Vampires can drink it cold, but I know from observing Adrian that he prefers his warm or room temperature.

Super gross, but here we are.

I try not to think about it when it's done heating, and I pour it into a large glass. I pretend that the coppery scent is actually sea salt and that the red is tomato juice. It does *not* work. I hold my breath and go knock on Adrian's door. He doesn't answer, but he left it unlocked, so I push it open and tiptoe inside. The lamp is on and he's laying on the bed, his eyes trained on the ceiling. He's wearing nothing but basketball shorts. I've only ever seen him in dress clothes, and it's hard not to stare at his body. His muscles are lean and strong, his shoulders are broad, and his skin is perfect without a single blemish. His golden locks are curlier than normal, like he's run his hands through them a million times. Those bright blue eyes track me as I walk in and set the glass on the nightstand.

He doesn't look at it, he looks at me.

"I'm sorry about Kelly," I say at last.

He sighs. "Do you know why I chose her?"

I shake my head.

"I rarely turn anyone into a vampire." His voice is faraway. "It's not a life I would condemn to anyone, despite what you might think."

"I don't know what I think anymore."

He's quiet for a while and then picks the conversation back up. "I met Kelly after she'd been attacked by one of my brothers. He left her for dead. I was going to end it for her, put her out of her misery. She begged me not to."

"So you turned her?"

"Not right away. Plenty of people beg for death, for life, or to make it stop. I was used to that."

"So what was different about her?"

"I knew her," he says simply, "she'd been someone else's fledgling for years, trying to get turned. I despised her for it, as I do all of them. I only take a child when my queen demands it."

"So Brisa demanded you take her?"

"Not that time. I did it to spite the brother who'd promised to turn her only to leave her for dead." He laughs bitterly. "Don't pretend to be surprised. You know how much I hated Hugo. I've had several enemies over the years, but he was perhaps my least favorite."

I don't expect this. I assumed he picked her because he liked her, not because he wanted to spite the brother who meant to kill her, to spite Hugo. "So I bit her, making sure my venom was strongest, and then I buried her and made her mine. The next time I saw him and she was on my arm, the look on his face was worth the effort."

My stomach sours, and I sit down on the edge of the bed. "You like to play games with people, don't you?"

He shrugs. "Sometimes. But I'm glad I turned Kelly.

She proved her loyalty and became my closest friend over the years. I could trust her with anything. And when we were assigned to New Orleans, she offered to be my assistant. She didn't have to. I could've gotten almost anyone for that job, but I trusted her the most with the inner-workings of my day, so I was grateful she offered." His voice goes ragged. "She deserved better."

"I'm sorry."

He sits up and takes the glass of blood in his hands, scowling down at it. "Sometimes, when I'm angry with myself, I don't eat."

Well, damn. There's some serious self-loathing going on here. I never expected it from Adrian of all people. And I never expected to feel bad for a vampire, but I do. I reach over and place my hand on his back. It's cold, but I don't flinch. "It doesn't do you any good to starve yourself. If anything, it makes you more dangerous to innocent people."

He doesn't respond, but he drinks, downing the glass in one go.

His lips are stained red when he turns to me. I drop my hand and take a deep breath. "There's something I need to talk to you about . . . Is there a coven meeting tomorrow?"

His eyes narrow, and he nods. "How did you know that? It's not for fledglings."

"You must have a spy somewhere in your organization because I didn't know that, Tate knew it."

His mouth curls and his eyes brighten, as if lights are

being turned on in his head.

"What *is* Tate?" I ask, growing desperate.

He doesn't answer. He sets the glass down and goes to his bathroom. He keeps the door open and turns on the shower.

"Come talk to me while I get ready," he says, "it sounds like we have a lot to discuss."

Okay, I've never seen a man shower before, and he probably knows that. But he's acting like he's back to business as usual.

"Don't get any ideas." I fold my arms over my chest.

"Oh please, Angel. I can get willing partners anytime I want and I've never been a prude about nudity. I am Greek, remember? But if you're uncomfortable, we can discuss this later. It's no problem."

I don't have time for later. I want to do this now. "Fine." I go sit on the bathroom counter and close my eyes. "But I'm not peeking."

He chuckles, and a few seconds later I can hear the shower door open and shut.

"So, tell me what Tate is?" I say, "And why are you enemies with him?"

"I cannot speak about what he is as my master has expressly forbidden it." His silky voice mixes with the steam. "But I will say that he and his kind are my enemy."

"They take energy from humans. That I do know." He doesn't reply. Maybe he can't. "Okay, so he's got this plan to send the hunters to ambush you at your coven meeting. His number one goal is to have you killed. I don't think he really cares all that much about what happens to the hunters."

"He's been after me for years," Adrian says. "He can't compel people, but if he could, I'd be fighting off humans every day."

I'd wondered about that with Cameron. I guess I know my answer.

"Don't worry, Angel. He won't succeed. If he wants me dead, he'll have to face me himself."

"So why doesn't he?"

"Because he knows he can't defeat a vampire with skills such as mine."

Adrian can levitate, aka fly, and has telekinesis, plus he's able to compel humans. He may have other abilities, too.

"So call off the coven meeting," I say. The room is thick with steam now; it coats me like a second skin. I carefully open my eyes, looking at my feet. My curious eyes want to travel to the glass shower, but I don't let them. Why does Adrian have to be so distracting? This would be easier if he were hideous.

"Why would I call off the meeting?" His voice grows angry. "Thanks to this insider information, I can kill the hunters. This is a good thing for my coven, not a bad one."

I stand, my hands fisting. "That's not why I told you this and you know it."

"So?" He steps from the shower, completely naked

and dripping wet. I don't look down nor do I blush. I glare at him, keeping my eyes on his, and he glares right back. "Your hunter killed Kelly."

"Cameron killed Kelly because he was confused."

"How was he confused?" Adrian seethes. "He used her to get closer to me. He failed to kill me, but managed to kill her. That's what happened."

"Cameron hated Tate," I shoot back, "but Tate messed with his mind and made him forget all about that."

"More reason to kill Tate's little hunters."

"So he can just make more of them? Because he will. You're not mad at the hunters. They're humans trying to protect their families. You're mad at Tate. Go after Tate."

"Maybe I'll use one of the hunters to get to Tate."

"How? They're all too young to be compelled."

He growls a little and grabs a towel, storming from the bathroom. I'm assuming he's going to his closet to get changed. I stay behind to cool off, even though the bathroom is sticky hot with condensation. I lean over the bathroom sink and wipe away at the mirror, staring at myself. I look tired. I look angry. Defeated.

No.

I won't let this defeat me. I can't give up. If this is how it's going to be, if he's going to turn into the monster he is, then I have to warn my friends.

I make for the exit, power walking through the suite. But when I pull open the door, Adrian's hand slams it closed. "You're not going anywhere, Angel," he growls against my ear. "You're mine."

CHAPTER 17

*I*f there's an award for the world's most gullible idiot, engrave my name on it because I've officially proven myself worthy. I shouldn't have trusted Adrian with this kind of information. My stupid plan to get deeper into the vampire organization and somehow save the world has completely backfired and soon my friends will be dead.

Not to mention, Adrian's grieving Kelly's death, so of course he's not going to call off the coven meeting because I asked him to, not when this is the perfect opportunity for him to get revenge. He's going to come out ahead on the war between hunters and vampires, and it's very likely that my friends will get killed. And if not, well, they'll for sure be turned into the VEC who will imprison them since hunting vampires is illegal. No matter what happens, it's going to change everything. And it's all my fault.

Adrian picks me up and takes me to his spare bedroom, tossing me onto the bed like a sack of potatoes. "Hand it over," he demands.

I glare and jump up before sprinting to the door. He blocks me. "Give me your phone," he seethes, "and your stake while you're at it."

I know better than to argue about having a stake, he knows I always carry one. I'm wearing long linen pants today that hang wide around my legs. The stake is strapped to my calf underneath. My phone is in my handbag, which happens to be in his kitchen. I'd forgotten all about it when I ran for the door. I know that seems improbable for someone of my generation since our phones are like a fifth limb, but try running from a vampire and then come talk to me.

"Fine, I'll do it myself," he growls.

I scream in frustration as he grabs onto my pants and rips them clean off my body, the seams splitting apart with ease. So now I'm standing here in my underwear and t-shirt.

Just great.

I'm fast, my own senses speeding up to try and match his. When he reaches for the stake, I block him. It's like blocking a stone wall, and my forearm aches, but I hold strong.

"Do. Not. Touch. Me."

He laughs bitterly. "I told you exactly what I was and warned you never to forget."

And I didn't. Or maybe I did a little because I

trusted him. My mind fills with guilt, and he uses that moment to grab the stake. It's wooden and it's tipped in silver, but he's careful to avoid the silver. "I'll be disposing of this," he says. "Now, where is your phone?"

"In the kitchen. It's obviously not on me. What, do you want me to strip naked so you can make sure?"

He smirks. "Oh, Angel, don't be surprised if you strip naked for me all on your own one day."

"You're vile," I seethe between gritted teeth. "I would never."

"And you're staying here until I decide what to do with you." He steps through the doorway and slams the door shut, the lock clicking into place.

Panic hits me. I don't remember the lock being on the outside, but sure enough, when I pull on the handle it doesn't budge. Could he have added it? This man is truly sick.

"How could you?" I pound on the door. "I came to warn you, to help you, not to let you kill my friends."

But he doesn't reply, and a few seconds later, I hear the door to the outside hallway close.

So that's it?

No, that can't be it.

I close my eyes, willing all of Hugo's venom to surface, channeling it into me stronger than ever. I slam against the door, expecting it to break. It doesn't. I do it again. And again. Each time hurting myself more. I'm going to have bruises. I may even fracture something.

But I don't care. I have to get out of here. I have to warn the hunters.

I do it again. This time I lose my balance and my head accidentally gets most of the impact. My vision narrows and then fades to black.

I don't know how much time passes before I wake in a bundle of cold limbs on the floor. I pick myself up and wait and wait and wait. The only way to pass the time is to watch the world go by outside the tinted glass. At least there's water in the bathroom but I have a pounding headache and my stomach starts to growl for dinner. I desperately want out of here, but that's not going to happen, so instead, I stare at the city below. All those people out there, what would they do if they were me? Would they be able to think of a viable plan? I wish someone could see me, but I'm too high up, and the windows are too dark to see through, anyway. I'm stuck.

A prisoner.

And I'm at the mercy of the man I foolishly trusted. I have nobody to blame but myself. I knew what vampires were capable of, knew humans didn't really matter to them beyond a source of food. And still, look at what I did.

As it always does, the world keeps turning, and time keeps marching on. The evening fades to night, and then the blackness takes over--an endless night. I lay on the bed and stare at the ceiling until I eventually fall asleep.

Morning comes and I expect Adrian will stop by with food and I'll have an opportunity to beg him again or maybe a chance to escape.

But none of that happens.

The day stretches and my stomach turns hollow. At least I can drink from the sink so it's not like I'm going to die up here like my friends will tonight.

For most of the day I think of their faces, imagining what they're doing right now to prepare for the attack. I wonder what Felix thinks of me standing him up last night. Does he assume I didn't show up because I got cold feet about sleeping with him? Or does he suspect something is wrong? Maybe he and Kenton and Seth are looking for me right now. Maybe they've already figured it out and are confessing to Tate.

There's no way to know, and being helpless is destroying me.

Eventually, night descends, and I know this is it. Somewhere below me in the hotel, the coven is meeting. And somewhere outside, the hunters are gathering. Their directive is to storm the ballroom. They'll work in teams, killing as many vampires as they can, with Adrian as their number one target.

It will never work.

I pace the room with a racing heart for what feels like hours. The night grows darker and darker. At one point I hear movement in the suite. I jump up and go to the door. "Adrian? Is that you?"

The movement stops and then starts again.

"Please," I beg, banging on the door, "please don't do this."

"Eva?" The voice doesn't belong to Adrian. No, it belongs to the man I hate almost as much as Adrian: Tate.

"Yes!" I scream, hopefully he's here to save me. "Let me out!"

"I'm afraid I can't do that yet." A door slams and then there's nothing but silence. He left me here.

I lay on the bed and cry. What was he doing in here if not to help me? But he's gone and I'm alone. When there are no tears left and the salt warms my mouth and my cheeks are streaked raw with the aftermath, my eyes finally begin to close on their own. I don't like that. I refuse to go to sleep. How can I?

And yet . . . I do.

My dreams torment me. Nightmares that tumble, one into another, over and over. I see my friends dying. I see some of them being turned. I see blood. Anger. Fear. I hear it, smell it, feel it. It's like I'm there, but I'm not there.

I'm not there.

Felix appears before me. His eyes are lovely brown, and then they're murderous red. And then he's kissing me. Fangs cut at my lips. I pull back and scream.

"Eva," he says, his hands cupping my face, "I'm still me."

"No," I reply, but the word gets trapped in my throat.

"Wake up," he snaps. No, not him. Someone else . . .

The hand is still on my face--a cold hand.

My eyes flutter open, and I'm looking up into Adrian's glacial eyes. He's so close. Too close.

"Get off!" I scream, pushing him away. My strength has gathered while I slept, the senses coming back all at once. He flies back against the wall and falls.

He's quick to recover and brushes himself off, smiling. "It looks like you're starting to get used to that venom," he teases. "But you should be careful with that. If the wrong person finds out about it, you'll either be turned or you'll be dead."

I can still be turned? Of course, I can still be turned. "I'd rather die." I glare.

"Hmm, I thought you'd say that. Your little request to become my prodigy was a lie from the beginning." He sighs. "Well, do you want to know about your friends or not?"

I jump out of the blankets, not caring that I'm hardly dressed. "What happened?" My voice comes out like sandpaper. "Are they dead? What did you do to them?"

"Nobody is dead," he says, and I nearly burst into tears.

"Arrested?"

"Not that either."

"So, what happened?"

He pauses for a second, considering. "They showed up, and we detained them. They're being held downstairs." He runs his thumb along his bottom lip for a moment. "Eva, I need you to do something for me, something important. And if you do, I'll let them all go. It will be as if nothing ever happened."

I don't want to hear what this request is because I'm afraid I may already know, but I have to face it. "What do you want?"

"I want you to come to France with me."

I blink at him; this was the last thing I expected him to say. "What's in France?"

"Who's in France," he corrects. "Brisa. She wants to meet you. I need you to be on your best behavior."

"That's all?" My eyes narrow. I don't believe him. I never will.

"You're still my fledgling, in case you've forgotten. We're being called to go to France where . . ." He stares at me, eyes softening, "where I'm going to turn you."

I feel as if I'm sinking into the ground, as if I'm already being buried alive, as if I'm already dead. No. I can't agree. I can't go to France. I can't meet the vampire queen. And I can't become one of them.

But what other choice do I have? It's me or it's all of them.

"Do I have your word?" My voice is so much stronger than I feel, and I can't imagine how I'm managing it when I feel like I've been shattered into a million razor-edged pieces. "You will do no harm to any of the hunters? You will set them all free?"

"Yes."

"I'll agree only if you promise to do that right now."

"But––"

"No, Adrian. I mean it." I fold my arms over my chest and give him a hard stare.

"Take the deal or leave it," he replies stonily.

Anger seeps into my tone. "You'll give me nothing?"

"I need leverage to make sure you behave in France." He's such a logical creature and I hate him for it.

"We have to come to a compromise."

"Do we? Because I'm the one holding the aces."

I throw my hands up. "I'm so tired of all your stupid gambling sayings." We're at an impasse and I don't know what to do. I can't trust him, he's already proved that. There's no telling that he won't take me to France and turn me into his prodigy no matter what I agree to. He's used to getting whatever he wants. "Please," I whisper. I'm truly defeated this time. He's won.

"Fine," he spits out. "I'll release them when we get on the jet, but I need you to go along with this in France. There's so much more on the line than you realize and I can't have your bad attitude getting in the way."

I scoff. "I think giving you my life should be good enough."

"This isn't about your life," he says, "it's about so many others."

"What does that have to do with me?"

"I need to go where I've been called and I need to take you with me before someone kills me here."

I raise a brow. "But you've got the hunters detained."

"The princes are being killed across the continents. There are only three of us left."

"I didn't know…"

"Don't you think your little friend Leslie Tate has something to do with that? He didn't show up to the casino, by the way. He sent in all the humans, exactly as you said he would."

I swallow. Should I tell him that Tate was in his suite? But I don't want to give him a single thing extra, so I keep my secret and reach out my hand. "Give me your word, and I'll give you mine. That's going to have to be enough for you."

"I rather preferred the blood vow." He chuckles, but I don't find it amusing. There's no way I'm ever kissing this man again, especially not for a fake vow which he would've let me keep on believing was real if I hadn't figured it out.

"Really? Because I'd rather prefer honesty."

He shakes my hand.

CHAPTER 18

A couple hours later and it's time to leave. "I don't have a suitcase or my phone back or anything." I give him a pointed look. "And what about my job? I have shifts, you know. I can't leave them in a lurch and disappear. And my apartment? I have to pay rent soon."

He responds by holding out his hand. "You need to leave your necklace here and forget about everything else. It doesn't matter. You have a new life now."

"Maybe it doesn't matter to you but it does to me." My voice wobbles. "Can I at least call my Mom?"

He winces but shakes his head. "The necklace, Eva."

He didn't use my pet name. Somehow it makes this all the more real. And maybe it's stupid, but this little necklace is the only thing I have left.

"I'll put it in my safe," he offers. "It'll be fine, but you can't take a silver cross to meet Brisa. It's offensive to vampires. You already know that."

I unlatch it with a grumble of reluctance. He produces a glove from his back pocket so he can handle the silver. He takes it in his hands and studies it for a minute, his face unreadable. What does he think of the feathers on the back? I want to ask him what he knows of it, but keep my thoughts to myself.

He leaves and returns with a pile of clothes. "Those are some of my sweatpants and a t-shirt to keep you comfortable for the plane ride. You'll have everything provided for you once we arrive at the palace."

The palace.

I didn't know the royal vampires lived in a palace, though I guess it makes sense. They're pretty private about things when it comes to that––one big mystery that the world is equally fascinated with and horrified by.

I'm tired and broken, so I don't ask any more questions.

We take a private jet with UV-proof windows. It looks like the ones in the movies with plush seating and decadent catered food. The pilots are humans, and when we climb aboard, Adrian compels them to keep us as safe as possible. Vampires have enemies the world over, what better way to take a prince down than by plane crash?

"Prove it," I say when he comes back into the cabin.

He doesn't have to ask what I mean. He retrieves his phone and fiddles with it before handing it over. The screen shows what the cameras all over the casino are seeing right now. The hunters are walking out the front door, free and clear. Felix turns to look up at the camera almost like he knows I'm watching him.

And then he's gone.

I hand the phone back to Adrian and buckle myself into my seat. I have nothing to say and I'm only half relieved. It's not like I wanted to sacrifice myself.

The flight is boring and quiet. I devour the pre-catered food even though my stomach is in knots. When Adrian apologizes for forgetting to feed me, I throw a baguette at his head and tell him not to speak unless spoken to. He rolls his eyes but proceeds to work on his computer without acknowledging me again. I don't even have a phone to play games or read an ebook or even a television to keep me company. I'm stuck staring out the tinted window at the expanse of white and blue sky between restless naps and finishing off the food.

When we finally fly over Paris, I'm practically glued to the window. It's daytime––been light out for hours now, part of the wonders of transatlantic airline travel. I catch sight of the Eiffel Tower standing vigil over the winding river and smile to myself. The city is gorgeous, and I'd love to explore it one day. I have a feeling this won't be the trip. But if the vampires succeed in turning me, I guess I'll have an eternity to explore.

My smile falters as a tear slips down my cheek. I don't want to explore the world in darkness. I've always loved the sun--the light, the warmth, the energy. My freedom means more to me than just about anything else and now it's gone. I hope wherever my friends are, they're safe and not trying to come after me. As much as I'd love to be rescued, I can't have them in danger because of me and I don't want all this to be for nothing.

We're on the outskirts somewhere, and I'm not sure how we're going to get from here to wherever we're going in broad daylight. But the plane drives slowly along the tarmac and pulls into a massive building--a huge garage door closing behind us. We climb out and immediately get into a waiting car. It's sleek and black, with no windows in the back.

"No windows?" I turn on Adrian.

"It's bulletproof but there's always a higher risk with windows," Adrian says. "We'll also be surrounded by a detail of human armed forces. Nothing will happen to us. We'll be fine."

"I hope you're sure about that because this thing is obvious. Anyone wanting to hurt vampires will know one of you is in here. What cars don't have windows?"

He doesn't respond, probably because he knows I'm right. Expose a vamp to sunlight and that's it. What a perfect way to do it. I try to imagine it happening to Adrian, but my mind won't let me go there. He's a pawn in all this too, isn't he? A pawn I'll never forgive, but a pawn no less. I've only seen Brisa once through a video call, but I'll never forget her face. I wish I could kill her and have it all be over, but Sebastian made a lot of sense. If she dies the vampires will have too much freedom.

I climb inside and it's like a coffin in here.

"It's a good thing I'm not very claustrophobic," I complain. When Adrian locks us in from the inside and a strip of red LED lights along the ceiling immediately brightens the enclosed cab, I relax a little. There are two rows of leather seats facing each other. He takes one and I take the other and the car begins to drive.

I've avoided eye contact since leaving New Orleans. This time I let my gaze linger over him and don't hold anything back about how I'm feeling. I'm angry. I'm frustrated. I'm scared. And I'm also attracted to him, which I hate, but there it is.

He stares right back. Something grows between us, thick and confusing.

"I'm sorry," he whispers, breaking the silence.

I have nothing to say to that. I don't know if I even believe him. Maybe it doesn't matter anymore.

He leans forward and then something slams into the car, metal hitting the metal like a bomb, and we're flying. I'm simultaneously kicking myself for not putting on my seatbelt and trying to grab onto Adrian. He can't get hit by sunlight. We're suspended in air as the vehicle flips over and then rights itself again.

Everything stops and the red lights flicker and then turn off.

"Are you okay?" I ask.

He hisses but his hands are on me, running up and down my body.

"What are you doing?"

"Checking for injuries. Hold still."

"Dude, I'm fine," I say and he stops.

"But I can smell blood." His voice whispers through the dark, taking on a sinister quality.

"It's my head." I can feel something wet dripping down my forehead and wince when I try to touch it. "I really should've worn that seatbelt."

"The venom will heal it fast."

"Oh, nice perk. Now tell me, do you have any guns stashed in here? I'd like to be able to defend myself." I never thought I'd hunt the vampire hunters but I don't want to die today.

He growls low. "Why do you have to smell so good?"

"Are you serious right now? We're under attack, someone is obviously trying to kill you, and all you can think about is my blood?" I keep feeling around the seats but there's nothing of use. I hate that I can't see in here!

He groans in frustration and when my hand accidentally brushes his, he catches it and tugs me into his lap. He wraps his arms around me in a cage and I freeze. "One taste," he whispers in my ear, "I promise not to bite."

I elbow him in the chest. "Don't be a creep." But he doesn't laugh and he doesn't let me go. He's breathing hard, fighting the instinct to feed on my wound. He resisted before but this time we're in close proximity and he may be minutes away from dying. What's stopping him?

I should, but I don't fight back. I lean into him and can't reason away why part of me is completely okay with this, maybe even wants to see how he reacts. "Fine, but I swear if you bite me, I'm going to rip your head off."

He chuckles and then his mouth is pressing against my cheek and moving upwards. He stops when he reaches the blood, tongue trailing along a line, cold and hot intermixing. He groans with satisfaction.

Gunfire sounds outside and it seems to shake him from his task because he stops. I use that as my cue to peel away from him and find the other bench. Little pops blast into the side of the car but nothing has a chance of getting through so far.

Someone knocks on the side of the car. I want to unlock it and go out there, but I know I can't expose Adrian like that. A French voice says something I can't understand and Adrian replies.

"What happened?" I ask.

"Hunters," he offers with a little growl. "They're gone now and we're continuing on."

The engine starts and the lights brighten. "What did I say about this car again?" he asks. Under the lights I can see my blood on his lips. He smiles, licks them clean, and teases me with a wink. "What did I say?" he presses.

"That nothing would happen to us when clearly it just did."

"I said we'd be fine and we're fine."

I hold my hand to my head wound and glare. "Speak for yourself."

CHAPTER 19

"We're going to the palace of Versailles," he tells me. "Act impressed. Queen Brisa will love that. But don't be needy, she hates needy."

"You're kidding," I whisper. "Versailles?"

Adrian looks at me sidelong. "Brisa's been wanting to take up residence there since Louis XIV built it. She even infiltrated his court for a few years and nearly succeeded in her efforts."

"She really doesn't know how to let things go, does she?" I lean back and close my eyes, trying to sort through my thoughts.

"No." The single word speaks volumes. I need to be careful from this moment on, more so than I've been in the past. If I'm going to get out of here alive, I must pretend that I'm here because I want to be here. The last thing I need is to get locked up, or worse, murdered because Brisa figures out I'm full of shit and want nothing to do with her creepy little vampire family.

The car stops again. Adrian pulls out his phone and looks at something. "There's cameras on the car," he says. "We're in a garage. It's safe to get out."

I scoff. "Why didn't you use that before?"

His eyes flick to my forehead. "I was distracted."

Right …

My fingers play at the wound. It's mostly healed right now, but I'm a mess. "I can't walk in there like this."

"You're with me," he says, "you'll be fine." He wrenches open the door and steps out.

We're met by household staff, a mix of humans and vampires. A vampire greets us, bowing to Adrian. I've never seen anyone bow to him, not even at his own coven meeting. Things must be pretty formal here. The vampire eyes the mess of blood but doesn't say anything. Then he's back to Adrian again. "Your highness."

Adrian clears his throat. "Casper, you don't need to call me that. How many times have we been through this?"

The older looking vampire doesn't even bother to respond to that. He stays professional as ever. "I must apologize. As Brisa recently acquired our new palace, it's not fully renovated yet. There's not a lot of space for everyone during the daylight hours."

"I'm sure it's fine," Adrian mumbles. "Can you direct me to a shower, please? I'd like to freshen up before meeting with Brisa. I think Evangeline would like to as well, given her current state."

I shoot him a little glare but nod my agreement because I probably smell like garbage and I'd like nothing more than to scrub off the dried blood.

"Of course." Casper turns and leads us through an unmarked door, then down a wide hallway and a sweeping staircase. "Most of the windows are boarded over as a temporary measure until we can get them all turned into bulletproof UV-proof glass." I bite my tongue from saying what a shame that will be. The building is stunning, even from the tiny slice we've seen so far. I'd love to explore it in all its grandeur sans tinted glass, and now I never will, not really, not now that the vampires have already started modifying it.

"Here you are." Casper's voice is apologetic. "Again, I'm truly sorry for the lack of space, but we did outfit the closets for you."

A human woman opens two large wardrobes which are bursting with clothes––but not modern day clothes. This is the stuff of fairy tales. "I'll be your personal maidservant." She smiles at me. "I'm Remi."

The vampire shoots her a pointed look and she rushes from the room. I think I like her—I don't like him.

"As I was saying, Her Majesty doesn't want any of the princes staying in the rooms with the boarded up windows. You are to be in the rooms with the new ones already installed. Oh, and don't be alarmed by the increase in guards when you roam about the palace. They're there for your protection."

"Thank you," Adrian cuts him off. "Don't worry. We'll be fine"

Casper leaves us to it, and we take in the room. It must've been a guest room from long ago, much of the decor has been meticulously cared for over the centuries. Either that or restored, because it looks like we could've time traveled right into France during the seventeenth century. I seriously hope the bathroom has running water. It must, because Casper probably would've said otherwise about the showers.

There's a grand four-poster bed in the center of the room with a loveseat and dressing table by the tinted window. Wallpaper lines the walls in textured blue and gold fleur-de-lis designs, and the crown molding is at least six inches thick.

Adrian strides over to the armoires and grumbles at the contents inside the one clearly meant for a man. "So she wants to play dress-up, does she?"

"What do you mean?" I join him, my heart squeezing when I get a better look at what's inside. The gowns are from what I think is the Renaissance age, or whatever age it was that this palace was built. I should've paid more attention in history class, not that we went into European history all that much in school. His clothing is in a similar fashion. I spend a good five minutes looking through all mine and then move to his. It reminds me of the princes from movies and television shows. "Wait a second," I let out a little snort, "do you have to wear tights?"

"They're called hose," he grumbles and I laugh again. "Excellent."

But really, I'm only teasing because the outfits are pretty cool.

"Admittedly, this wasn't my favorite era for fashion," he says.

"And what is?"

"Nice form fitted suits from a tailor as you often see me in or as close as I can get to nudity, take your pick."

I punch him in the arm. "Ew, did you really have to go there?"

"It's the truth. I don't like to feel constricted."

And wearing a suit isn't constricting? I roll my eyes. And then my mouth pops open when I finally put the pieces together that Adrian and I are sharing this little room. It's not that big of a deal, it's not like vampires sleep, but it still feels way too intimate. I'm only here because he blackmailed me into coming. My hatred for it all is no surprise, and I hate him too for manipulating me. And now I'll have to be turned into one of them while wearing a massive ball gown.

I carefully close the armoires and spin around to plead with Adrian. "You can't turn me." My voice wobbles. "Please."

"We have a deal."

"One I was manipulated into making."

"I don't want to turn you, Angel, but I have to follow her orders." He looks away.

"Please. Promise me you'll at least try to save me from it."

"Vampires can't promise anything, least of all me." He walks to the bathroom. "Don't try to run away. You'll be killed if you do."

He closes the door, and I fall back onto the bed, staring up at the canopy over the bed. There's no way this is happening. There's no way. It can't be.

But it is.

After Adrian finishes in the bathroom, I go inside. Turns out there's no shower in this room, but there is a beautiful clawfoot bathtub. I soak in it until my fingers turn to prunes, and the blood on my scalp is gone, then I slip into silk pajamas––the only thing that's not a dress–– while I'm still in the bathroom because I desperately want to get out of Adrian's sweatpants and do so in privacy. I come back out into the bedroom to find Adrian lying on the bed with his hands behind his head and his eyes closed. I know he's not sleeping but perhaps he's resting his mind. All the more reason to disturb him.

I stomp through the room, throwing the old clothes down next to the armoire because I have no idea where else to put them, and settle into the couch. This isn't an enemies-to-lovers, only one bed, will-they won't-they situation. This is an enemies-to-allies-to-enemies, and I refuse to go near that bed when he's on it.

"You know," I say loudly, hoping to disturb him, "the least you could do is let me enjoy one last hurrah in the daylight." It's late afternoon, and there may only be a few hours left for me. Adrian doesn't move. "What would you give to have one more hour in the sun?"

His eyes open, and he peers over at me.

"Well?" I fold my arms over my chest and raise my eyebrows.

"I'd do anything."

"Exactly." I nod toward the door. "Do you think I care about those guards out there? Give them an excuse and help me get outside."

"You're not leaving this palace during the sunlight and it's not your last night as a human."

"You don't know that," I say sharply, "and I don't appreciate being lied to anymore."

He sits up and runs his hands over his face. "You're right. I don't know that. But I do know that Brisa will want to test you for a while first. I also know that if she thinks for even one minute that you're not loyal to me, and thus to her, then you won't be turned. You'll be dead."

"And what does sunlight have to do with that?"

He flashes through the room so quickly I nearly fall off the loveseat. He's on his knees, leaning over me. I'm average height, but he's tall, and he dwarfs me in both his size and his presence. His fangs extend, and fear seizes me. I have no way to protect myself. "The sun has everything to do with that. You should want this so bad that you'd be eager to throw away the sun. You should worship the darkness. And if Brisa suspects how you really feel, I can promise you'll be wishing you were dead."

"But you said she'd kill me." Okay, now I'm just being a smart ass.

"She will, but she won't hurry to do it. She'll take her time. And then she'll go after your family and anyone you've loved." His eyes flash silver. "The last person you want to cross is a vampire, and Brisa is the worst of them all."

"Sebastian said there were worse ones than her." There I go again.

He stills. And then he stands. "There may be." He starts to pace the room. "Someone has been killing off princes, and when they can take over those bloodlines, they will target Brisa next. I know vampires that would like nothing more than to enslave the human race. Hugo was one of those. I suspect Sebastian is as well, though I don't know for sure; he's always been disgustingly loyal to Brisa."

"And so have you."

He nods, but he knows what I mean. He's loyal to her as a defense mechanism. There's a knock on the door, and Adrian opens it. "Sorry to interrupt," a woman says, "but we're to get her ready for the ball."

"Is that you Remi?" I ask, strolling to the door, grateful to find a human and not another vamp.

"Yes, Miss."

"The ball?" Adrian frowns. "Are we seriously doing one of those again?" He sounds as if he's a duke and a million mamas are after his hand for their eligible daughters. I fail to bite back a laugh.

"Oh yes. Queen Brisa insisted we have one every night the first year she's here." First year? Remi looks pointedly at me. "Come along now, there's much to do."

CHAPTER 20

I stop laughing abruptly. This is so not my scene. But I have to play the part, that much Adrian has made clear. I really hope that I can trust him this time. I snort again and he shakes his head.

"Lord help us all," he moans.

The young woman looks to be in her twenties—probably old enough to be compelled so she can work here. She takes me to a dressing room, and I'm descended upon by five other human women of varying ages. I seriously wonder if they work here because they want to or if they're here because they've been compelled. I wouldn't be surprised by either. Too many humans have accepted vampires as part of everyday life. We've become complacent and desensitized, treating vampires like part of society instead of a stain on it. Maybe the vamps pay well? They certainly have the money.

The maidservants don't make me bathe again, but they do my nails, style my hair onto the top of my head, apply way too much makeup, and then fit me into a corset that makes my waist tiny and my boobs big. Then comes the heaviest gown I've ever worn, times a million. "What is this thing?" I complain, already getting hot. It's itchy and huge. It's also a striking sapphire blue that compliments my tanned skin tone. The bodice is cut in a low sweetheart shape, and the twins are on full display, having been pushed up by the ridiculous corset underneath. I think of Ayla, and my heart hurts. I'd love to share this with her, sans vampires of course. She would absolutely love it.

At least, the old her would have.

She still hates me. She knows I've dumped her brother but still doesn't want to talk to me. She hates that I joined the hunters but she doesn't seem to get that I'm doing it because I love her and want her to live in a safer world. If only I could text her.

"Do any of you have a phone?" I ask the ladies. They frown. "I want to take a picture of myself like this." I hold the universal symbol of phone to my ear by extending my thumb and pinky.

"*Non, Non,*" one of them says. "*C'est interdit!*"

"I'm sorry, I don't speak French."

"She said it is forbidden. Privacy is of the utmost importance here," another replies, speaking English with a thick French accent, "there are no phones allowed in the city for us humans."

"So what do you tell your families when you get home? Do they know you work here?"

"We live here," another supplies. She barely has an accent at all. "This is our home. We are each other's family now."

She sounds a little robotic, and I know the answer to my earlier question. These humans have been compelled, probably multiple times. The only one that seems to have any spirit left in her is Remi, but she keeps quiet about the phone thing, shooting me an apologetic look.

"Sorry," I mumble.

They finish off the job with white gold jewelry adorned with diamonds and sapphires. The sparkling jewels settle around my neck and hang off my ears like prison chains. And when it's time to go, I don't want to move.

Adrian meets me at the door. When he sees me all dolled up, his face darkens. "Get out," he commands the women. They scurry away, and then we're alone in the little windowless dressing room.

"Please," I ask one last time, "please don't make me do this."

When he doesn't respond, my breathing starts to speed up and my vision blurs. My hands begin shaking and waves of anxiety crash over my body, drowning me alive. "I can't . . . I can't breathe." My knees buckle, and Adrian catches me before I'm on the floor. He sits down and holds me in his lap, trying to shush me. I can barely even tell he's there. In a corner of my mind, I'm aware that I'm having a panic attack. I've never had one before, and they're as terrifying as people say. But even though I'm partially aware of what's going on, I can't seem to stop it, nor can I distance myself from it.

No, I'm stuck right here in the middle of it, forced to feel every bit. The more I think I can't breathe, the more it comes true. I claw at the back of my dress. I have to get out of the corset. I can't have something choking my lungs like this. My fingers fumble with the laces, but I'm completely stuck. "Get it off me," I beg, tears streaming down my face.

In one quick move, Adrian rips the back of the dress completely in two and then the corset underneath. The sound of fabric tearing is right here but it's also like it's a million miles away. Everything slows and then speeds up as I'm freed from the gown. I scramble out of it, wearing only the cream slip the ladies use for under-wear here. I gasp for breath and let it filter through me.

I lie back on the floor.

"Here," he says, lifting my knees up, "try to talk to me. What's your favorite color?"

The question is so out of left field it catches me off guard a little. "Umm." I swallow hard, trying to clear the panicked haze from my mind. "Green."

"Any particular shade?"

"Nature. Any green that comes from nature."

"Good choice," he replies, "I feel that way about all colors."

Except he can't see nature anymore, unless it's in the dark. And who would want to go enjoy everything our beautiful planet has to offer in the middle of the night? Something nags at me, a memory from his penthouse suite. "Is that why you always have a bouquet of fresh flowers in your living room?"

"I enjoy it how I can, even if it means killing it first."

I sit up, my breathing finally stabilized. "Spoken like a true vampire."

"I have a plan, you know," he says, "I don't want to turn you, either."

"So don't."

"I won't if I can help it. Like I said, I have a plan."

"So tell me about it." My voice cracks.

"I can't tell you everything," he says, "it's not safe for you to know. But I'll tell you that Brisa likes us to use the catacombs for the business of making our prodigy. When we take you there, you have to stay for three days and nights."

I shiver, thinking of The Cask of Amontillado. We had to read the ominous short story by Edgar Allan Poe in high school about a man who buries someone alive in a catacomb. The final line was "in pace requiescat," which our teacher said meant "may he Rest In Peace." Yeah, guy was still alive in there!

No, thank you.

"But what about Hugo's venom?" My heart squeezes. "Will I be yours?"

He shakes his head. "This isn't easy for me to

explain." He grimaces in pain. He's fighting whatever it is that keeps him from going against his maker's wishes, and when he speaks again, it's through gritted teeth. "You'd have to be down there for three days and nights before you'd rise as one of us. Sometimes vampires can rise a little early or a little late, and they're still one of us, but they may be a little weaker or even stronger. Three days, though. Remember that number."

He won't say more but I can tell he wants to.

"What if someone were to be able to leave before their time was up?"

He opens and closes his mouth, then groans in frustration. He can't speak it. So I'll say it for him.

"Would they stay human?" I study his face as memories flood him.

He nods and then shakes his head. "They'd be human, but they'd have . . ."

"Heightened senses," I whisper.

He just looks at me, but I know what he's trying to say and something loosens in my chest. I take a deep breath and think back to my own experience. "Heightened senses and an ability to be able to hunt down the vampires in that bloodline."

Because I'd done it before. That's how I was able to kill Hugo's children so easily.

And then Hugo himself.

Sure it had been a fight, but if I hadn't had that venom, I would've been far more disadvantaged.

"I can see why this information is a guarded secret among your kind."

He gives me a hard look. "And if it were to get out and be traced back to me, I'd face the true death. Brisa wouldn't stake me either. That's too clean. She'd most likely put me out in the sun to burn alive."

He's trusting me with something that he shouldn't. I mop up my tears and straighten my shoulders as I speak. "I don't understand why you're telling me all this. You used my friends against me to blackmail me into coming here and get me to agree to be turned, and now you're telling me how to get out."

"Things aren't always what they seem," he says.

I roll my eyes. "Seriously? That's your answer?"

"It's time to go." He stands and helps me up, looking me square in the eyes. "Please go along with whatever Brisa says. You must. If you don't, we'll both die."

"What did she do to you?" The question I've been dying to ask for weeks finally bursts out. I know the bloodlines make it so he has to obey her commands, but there's more to the story. I see it in his eyes every time he speaks of her.

Adrian *hates* Brisa. It's a loathing that I've never seen before.

His shoulders go rigid, and he glares at me as he speaks. "Brisa is charming and beautiful, but never forget that she's cunning and cruel."

"You can tell me," I say softly. I take his hand in mine and squeeze. I don't know what's come over me, maybe it's the lack of oxygen to my brain or something, but I want to comfort him.

"She never gave me the choice to be her prodigy," he bites out, "and I will do everything in my power to make sure I never do the same to another human." But there's got to be more. I drop his hand, willing to let the conversation go, but he keeps talking. This time he doesn't look at me. "I woke up in darkness. I didn't know what had happened to me. I was so thirsty and confused. I dug my way out from my grave and stumbled home. When I got there, my wife was asleep in our bed and I––" His voice cracks, and he doesn't say anything more. He doesn't have to. I already know.

Adrian killed her.

But it wasn't his fault, not really. He'd been turned without even knowing what a vampire was and had no direction or help from his master when he awoke.

"She was pregnant," he continues, and my heart drops. "Brisa found me later that night and made me think she was helping me. For years, I didn't understand what had really happened. But when I eventually lifted out of the bloodlust, I knew what a monster I was. And I knew it was because of her."

I would hate her too. "You're not a monster," I lie. And maybe it's not totally a lie. Like he said, things aren't always as they seem.

He finally looks back up at me. "Don't worry, Angel. I don't need you to make me feel better, but I do need you to do this for me. We're going to this ball tonight, and tomorrow, and every night we have to, and when Brisa decides it's time, I turn you. You will lay in your grave, and you will act happy about it. And if you do those things, I'll do everything in my power to make sure you don't stay down there for three nights."

"I thought you said vampires can't make promises."

"We can't."

CHAPTER 21

he servants have to get me dressed again. I expect them to be upset, but they're not. They don't really seem to have many emotions at all. I wish I could free them from this place, and maybe someday I will.

I want to kill Brisa.

So badly.

I know that it's not a smart idea, that cutting the head off the snake will breed many more with even worse venom, but I hate that I can't just drive a stake through her heart and end her tyranny over her "children" and so many others.

I force all of that to the back of my mind as I prepare for what comes next. The servants keep the jewels on me, but choose a silver gown instead. At first, I think it's not as pretty as the blue one, but once it's on and I look in a gilded mirror, I change my mind. I'm dressed like a winter princess. It's not my style in the slightest, but considering how drafty and cold the palace is, I decide to count it as a blessing.

"I got this for you," Remi says, handing me a notebook and pencil. "It's not much but it's a drawing pad. You can use it to sketch or journal. Whatever you want during the times you're not otherwise occupied."

It's a small gesture but it means everything. "Thank you," I say, wrapping her into a hug with the book between us. "Will you put it in my room for me?"

"It's locked," she says sheepishly, stepping away. We're probably not supposed to hug given the way Casper glared at her for speaking out of turn. "Adrianos has made it very clear that nobody else is allowed in there. I'm not even sure he'll give you a key."

"Oh, he will," I supply, "I'll make him."

Her smile quirks and she takes the notebook and pencil back. "Either way, I'll leave these here and you can come back tomorrow to find them. Right now it's time to go meet the queen."

I swallow hard and nod. Remi offers a smile of assurance but I catch the sheen of worry in her hazel eyes. Her hair is tucked up into a bonnet, her would-be curly blonde locks hidden away. I need a friend here––I feel so alone––but I'm not sure it's safe for anyone to be my friend at this point. All I do is bring friends down and put them into danger.

Adrian is back to his stoic self when I'm ushered into the hallway. He doesn't say a word about my appearance, and I don't about his either. He's heartbreakingly, earthshatteringly beautiful. And I'm aware "earthshatteringly" isn't even a word. But it is one in my book now, and right next to it is a picture of Adrianos Freaking Teresi.

It's not fair that he makes it so easy to hate him while simultaneously making it hard.

The orchestra music, melodic and sweet, leads us to the ballroom, and we enter with our heads held high.

My hackles rise instantly. Vampires of all ages, shapes, and ethnicities are scattered throughout. More than I've ever seen in one place! They watch me with hungry eyes, and, for the gazillionth time, I'm reminded of my virginity. It's not like it's hard to go find some willing guy to lose it with, but I'd been holding out for someone I love. I thought I loved Felix. Maybe I still do love Felix. But I'm not sure we'll ever find the right timing.

The crowd splits like Moses parting the Red Sea as we head toward Brisa. The queen is like a beacon unto herself—everything about her glows. From her warm-honey colored hair, to her sparkling eyes, soft skin, hourglass figure, and the natural way she carries herself—commanding the room with both power and grace, Queen Brisa is everything I'd imagine a vampire queen to be.

She's surrounded by what I can only assume are guards. They are vampires dressed in all black garb, and their eyes constantly scan the room. They have huge guns. I've never seen vampires with guns before but it makes sense. Vampires can't be killed with bullets, but humans certainly can. And who are their enemies if not humans?

And whatever the energy demons are——maybe guns can kill them too. One day, I will find out what Tate is, and I will find out how to protect my friends from whatever his kind is. Tate won't get away with continuing to put innocent young human lives at risk for his own goals. But right now, I have to focus on Brisa. As we approach, I dress myself in my most winning smile and cling tighter to Adrian's arm. I want her to think I'm enamoured with him, with this life——the true mark of a fledgling.

Brisa turns, as if sensing I'm there, and looks right into my eyes. Her gaze is mesmerizing, locking me in like a hypnotist. Her posture hardens, and her mouth frowns for a second. Is she jealous? Territorial? Hard to please? Maybe I shouldn't hang off of Adrian. I relax my arm and slip away from his hold. Brisa notes the move and tilts her head at me, as if studying that too.

I wonder what kind of abilities she has, what her strengths and weaknesses are. If Adrian can levitate, can move objects with his mind, and can compel humans better than most other vampires, then what does the queen have in her arsenal besides her obvious power over the bloodlines?

"There she is." Her voice is smooth like butter, with a silky hint of a French accent. "I've been looking forward to meeting the girl who's convinced my Adrian to add to our family again."

"Hello." My voice comes out too nasally. I offer a curtsy. "Your Highness."

"Hello to you too, Mother," Adrian's voice is light and playful. It's nothing I've heard from him, it has to be fake, and I almost lose my nerve right then and there. "Please, don't forget about my Kelly so soon."

She hugs him, her arms slipping around his neck. "How could I? She was a lovely woman who will be missed." She steps back, her voice growing icy. "It's a real shame those hunters in New Orleans have grown so strong lately, Adrian. How many deaths are there now? By my count, you've lost six vampires from your coven in less than two months."

He frowns at that and she turns to me. "You wouldn't happen to know anything about that, would you, Evangeline?"

Can she tell if I lie? Will my heart speed? I don't know what to do because I don't know how much Adrian has told her, but Sabastain came on her errand. So she must know enough by now. I can't lie to her.

But before I can speak, Adrian cuts her off. "Mother, you know Evangeline has infiltrated the hunters for us. She happens to be an old friend of one of them and convinced him to bring her into their organization. She's spying on that vile Leslie Tate for me."

Well, that answers that. I nod in agreement, hating

that my cheeks are burning the entire time. I always thought I could play it cool, and then I met vampires.

"And what have you learned of Leslie Tate?" she asks me.

"I know that he wants Adrian dead," I say, gaining courage, "and I know that you've lost some of your princes recently, haven't you? I'd wager that Tate and his organization have played a large part in that. In fact, Tate left for a little while last month and didn't tell anyone where he went. When did you say your sons died?"

The question hangs between us for far longer than I'd like. "Very astute observation," she says at last, and then she waves us away. "But this is supposed to be a party. Please, go enjoy yourselves."

We're dismissed for now.

So we end up dancing and trying to enjoy the party, as per Brisa's wishes. It's not easy for me, but Adrian lets himself relax in a way I haven't seen before. I think back to Brisa's instructions and wonder how far her commands reach into these people. If she told them all to go jump off a bridge or to walk out into sunlight, would they?

Adrian introduces me to the vampires who inquire after us--a sea of beautiful new faces--but otherwise it's just the two of us. He's probably used to coming to these things with Kelly, and I wonder what he thinks about being here with me.

"What's that look on your face for?" he asks, pulling

me against him for a slow dance. We sway to the music, and I'm surrounded by him to the point that I can hardly think. "This is supposed to be fun."

I sigh. "You know this isn't easy for me."

He nods once. "But you're doing a good job."

"When do you think it's going to happen?" He doesn't have to ask what I mean. All I can think about is the turning ceremony and being taken underground in those catacombs, laying among a bunch of old bones. I want to scream just thinking about it.

"I don't know. Could be tonight, could be tomorrow, could be in a month from now."

A month! "How long are we going to be here?" I swallow hard.

"As long as she wishes. Time is different to vampires, especially one as old as our queen."

I sneak glances at the others as we dance. Everyone is dressed in the same fashion, like we've traveled back in time. The other guests occasionally look our way, but mostly keep their distance and mingle amongst themselves. I wonder what kind of reputation Adrian has. He's a prince, so he's important, but that's all I know.

"I haven't even gotten to say goodbye to my mom," I whisper. "I want my phone back."

"Your phone is in New Orleans." He pulls me even closer until our bodies are flush against each other. "You already know Brisa doesn't like technology."

"That's pretty hypocritical--"

He cuts me off, literally putting a hand to my mouth.

My eyes go wide at the fury in his expression. "Come." He leads me from the ballroom and out into the midnight courtyard. Even in the darkness, it's stunning and smells like fresh spring flowers despite it being early October. There are lawns that seem to go on forever, and more gardens than I could possibly count. Off in the distance, a shoulder-height hedge maze weaves endlessly. Party guests roam about out here, some couples finding the darkest corners, but most have stayed inside where the action is.

He keeps walking me out until we're well away from the glitter of lights. "There are listening ears everywhere," he says, voice dark and low, "so I will only say this once."

CHAPTER 22

"Your mother is safe," he continues, "and your friends are fine. If you wish to have a life as a human, you'd better listen closely. It's not going to be easy and I can't promise you anything. But I will try my best. If I'm to succeed, you must go along with everything I ask of you." He squeezes my hands. "One misstep and you're dead."

I let out a frustrated breath. "Fine."

"Brisa is living out a fantasy right now. She's been trying to gain control of this palace for ages, and now that she has, she wants to pretend she's Marie Antoinette for a little while."

"Didn't Marie's own people assassinate her?"

His eyes flash. "You know the story then."

Is he trying to tell me something? I step back and he drops my hands. "Yeah, let them eat cake and all that."

"Brisa won't even let *me* have a phone here. She's

decided that she's the only one who can have access to the outside world, at least for now. She's paranoid about someone trying to usurp her. This is as much a test of me as it is for you."

"But don't you have business to run in New Orleans? You can't hang around here."

"I do," he grits out, "so let's get through this as quickly as possible so we can get back to our lives."

His life. Not mine.

He drags me back to the party and I put on my best show. I smile happily and chat with everyone, though never leaving Adrian's side. We act as if we're more than friends, as if we're in the process of falling madly in love, holding hands constantly, dancing too close, his arm or hand never straying from my body for even a second, his lips grazing my cheek or nuzzling into my neck. Everyone seems to buy it, and for a few moments throughout the night, I buy it too.

And that scares me, because I don't always know what's real and what's fake with Adrian. I know what my head wants--to get out of here. But my body betrays me, enjoying every touch. And my heart? I don't even let myself go there.

We're in the middle of chatting with a group of vampires who are sucking up to Adrian--vampires sure are good at that--when a couple strolls into the ballroom and everyone quiets down. We're all watching them with rapt attention, and I can't blame anyone, can't even blame myself.

They are hands down the most beautiful couple I've ever laid eyes on--and also the most in love. I can tell by the way they look at each other, the way they hold each other's hand, and the glow in their eyes. They're absolutely mad for one another. I didn't know vampires could feel that way and the realization makes me feel a little conflicted.

"Who's that?" I find myself asking. The woman looks Japanese with glossy long black hair that curls and shears off at her waist. Her beauty could rival Brisa's on a bad day. The man is her equal, with coppery-blond hair that spans to his chin, broad shoulders, and a uniquely masculine face--he could be a model for a cologne commercial. "He kind of looks like a Viking," I add.

"That's because Magnus was a Viking," Adrian replies. "And Katerina is his wife."

There's a subtle shift in the air when the couple greets the queen. I wish I could listen in on their conversation, because from here it looks like Brisa doesn't like Katerina one bit.

Adrian takes my hand and leads me through the crowd toward the couple, whispering in my ear as we move. "Magnus is another of Brisa's princes. We aren't allowed to marry, but he met Kat during the Second World War and brought her back to our mother, and insisted they make it official. It was a scandal, but Brisa eventually agreed to let them wed."

"That's romantic," I hear myself saying. No, it's not! Kat's a vampire now.

"Make no mistake, they have fallen out of favor with the queen and have spent the years since trying to prove themselves. Let's just say they still have a long way to go."

I wonder how they're even alive. Adrian makes it sound like Brisa gets her way no matter what. The exception she made for Magnus must have caused a huge upset in her court.

"My brother!" Adrian turns on the charm as we approach, slapping the Viking on the back. I wonder how much of this is real, but Adrian does seem happier around Magnus than he ever did with Sebestian or Hugo. "It's been too long. What have you been up to?"

"They've been helping me," Brisa interrupts and everyone gives her their complete attention. "Traveling, and such." She waves her hand around vaguely. I thought all the princes ran different areas of the world and find this interesting--likely another blow to the couple.

Magnus is one of the last princes left right now and I wonder what that will mean for him and Katerina. Maybe they'll be brought back into favor simply because they're the only ones still standing. Or maybe Brisa will make more children, giving them better roles to spite Magnus. But I don't see any fledglings around Brisa and I haven't all night.

"It's good to see you happy, Adrianos." Brisa's rich voice turns on the two of us.

"Thank you, Mother."

She smiles and my hackles rise. There's something amiss in her expression. Her gaze turns to Adrian. "Come to my chambers with me, please. We have some catching up to do."

"Always," he says, his tone going hollow.

I can't be certain of her meaning, but I think she is letting me know that even if Adrian and I were to be in a relationship, she still has the power. She can call him to her "chambers" at any time, and he will go. She's the one in control, and there's nothing I can do to stop her. Even killing her is off the table now that I know what the outcome would be.

She kisses my cheeks goodbye, reeking of fresh blood and roses. She doesn't pull away. Her fangs extend, and I freeze. She could bite me, and then what would happen? Would she know I already have vampire venom in my veins?

But she pulls away, taking Adrian's hand and wrapping it around her waist, sashaying from the room. He never looks back.

I'm a human girl alone in a room full of vampires. Most of them have taken lives like mine without a glimmer of remorse. Maybe all of them have. Brisa changed things in order to allow them to come out in public, but their base nature has stayed the same. If anything, my association with Adrian has proved that I can't forget what they are and I shouldn't trust them. I swallow hard, wanting to get away.

"She did the same to us before we were married," Katerina says, jarring me from my thoughts. I shake my head and she tilts hers. "Oh, are you and Adrian not together?"

"We're not like that. I'm his fledgling only."

"Hmm…" She raises a thin brow at her husband. "What do you think of this one, Magnus?"

He peers down his nose at me and I feel about two inches tall. The loving gaze he had for his wife has turned to one of cool indifference as he looks at me. "I liked Kelly better."

Shock prickles at my cheeks.

"Kelly was lovely. Such a shame." They turn and walk away, leaving me gaping.

What on Earth?

I don't know if I've ever been so openly insulted like that. And to think I instantly liked them at first! It goes to show that vampires may be attractive to us humans, but that doesn't mean they're something we should seek after. At the end of the day, we're food, sometimes potential servants or lovers or maybe even prodigies, but we're not on their level. And in their minds, we never will be.

I need to get out of here. The exit is on the other side of the vast ballroom and I start that way, but somehow end up being tugged into the dance floor. I'm nearly knocked to the marble floor and a group of vampires laugh as they trample over the hem of my gown.

Fakers! They acted as if they liked me when Adrian was around and now I'm nothing but a useless human for their cruel amusement. The stakes are higher than ever for me. One false move and I may end up dead. I guess that makes me a faker too.

"It's good to see you again." A voice purrs into my ear, and I spin around into Sebastian's arms. This is the first I've seen of him since the day we met. I step back involuntarily. "May I have this dance?" His lips quirk at the corner and he tugs me back in. "Don't worry, Adrian won't mind. He's not even here."

"What about Fiona?"

"Ah, that's right. I forgot you met her." He nods to another dancing couple and I catch sight of Fiona in a man's arms. "She's busy. Now let's dance."

Realizing people are watching us, I settle into his arms, and we begin to circle around the room in a waltz. I don't know what I'm doing, but he's an expert lead, his eyes never straying from my face. I don't say anything, I'm not sure what to say to this creature. The sight of him makes my skin crawl--he's too much like Hugo.

"Aren't you curious?" He tilts his head.

"About what?"

"About my findings," he continues. "You know I came to New Orleans to investigate the death of my brother--a death you witnessed."

I hold my chin high. "And what did you find?"

But really, I want to know how long he stayed in town and what else he did there. Was he part of the raid when the hunters tried to take down the coven a few nights ago? Because if so, he's bound to know too much about me. Or maybe not. I wasn't there and my story might still stand.

Maybe that's why Adrian locked me in his suite.

"You know, it's funny," he continues, his grip suddenly tight, "everyone I spoke with all denied having anything to do with my brother's death. But they certainly knew who you were."

His fangs extend, and his eyes flash murderous.

"It was hunters," I hurry to supply, "but none that I recognized." I mix lies with truth, hoping it all comes out sounding real. "Brisa and Adrian already know about me. I'm a spy for them. But you do realize there are other hunter groups in Louisiana, right?"

"I know you are lying," he hisses, "and the only thing keeping me from tearing your head off is an order from my queen to keep Adrian's pretty little new pet safe. You'd better be grateful to Brisa. She's the reason you're still breathing."

I try to pull away, but he keeps us spinning round and round the dance floor like a puppet master. And I'm nothing but a helpless doll. The crowd seems to have thickened, and the party has grown obnoxious since Brisa left. I need to get out of here. Faster and faster we go, my feet start to drag on the marble floors, the heels at an odd angle. My ankles scream in protest.

"You're hurting me," I squeal.

He stops abruptly and releases me. "I apologize. Sometimes I forget how weak you humans are." But I read between the lines. This is a threat, the equivalent of telling me to watch my back because he'll kill me if he gets the chance.

CHAPTER 23

*J*hurry back to the room and pray I don't meet any more vampires along the way. Even in low candlelight, the palace is stunning with tall ceilings painted with Renaissance scenes, intricate tapestries on the walls, and plush rugs underfoot. There is lovely furniture and every shade of gold, blue, and white imaginable decorating the open spaces. And pastels as far as the eye can see.

My outfit blends right in, even down to the slippers on my feet. They have tiny heels at the bottoms and clack softly as I walk. I wish I could enjoy this palace more, but it's impossible. I want to find a way out of here, but Adrian's right. There are too many guards and it's too risky. His plan is the only way, but it doesn't feel like much of a plan to me. More like a hope and a way to keep my mouth shut so Brisa stays happy.

Flickers of light lead the way since the place is lit up

solely with candles. Save for a few exceptions like running water, the guards with walkie-talkies, and I'm sure the Wi-Fi that Brisa uses, this place is authentic to the old French courts. Adrian said that Brisa infiltrated it for a while so she must know how things were done. She has one foot firmly planted in the past and one in the present day, allowing her to control her bloodlines while still living her life in the luxury she prefers. But at what cost? Someone has to pay for all this, and I'm not talking about the literal money the vampires have acquired over the years like mythical dragons hoarding piles of gold, I mean the countless lives that have been lost to Brisa's ambitions.

Outside, the black sky is giving way to the starless navy that comes minutes before sunrise. The vampires will be leaving the party now and retreating to safer places in the palace. They don't sleep, so I'm sure their celebrations will continue, but I'm ready for bed. I quicken my step, rounding the corner toward the room Adrian and I share.

But it's not the corner I thought it was.

And I don't know where my room is.

A wave of panic crashes over me the moment I realize I'm lost. I look around, desperate for a servant to help me. Surely they'll know every nook and cranny and can lead me to safety. But they're nowhere to be seen. Maybe they're smarter than I am. The vampires are retreating into the shadows, drunk on blood and rowdy. I can hear several yelling at each other through the halls.

I step into a darkened alcove and wait for them to pass, but they never do.

Nobody comes in this wing. Why is that?

In a book, this is where I'd stumble upon a secret passageway. It would lead me to uncovering a mystery, or even better, a way out of this palace.

Of course, that doesn't happen. I'm no heroine in some nicely laid out story. I'm nothing but a weak and foolish girl who keeps making mistakes. I never should've agreed to come here. A smarter person would've figured out how to save her friends and get away from the vampires. Better yet, a smarter person would have avoided the vampires from the very beginning. But I'm not that person. I'm the girl whose dad died when she was a kid, the girl who had trouble making friends until she found the one true friend that mattered. And then I lost her, too. I'm the girl who got herself bit by vampires and ended up here because of it.

But maybe I need to stop blaming myself. Maybe I was taken advantage of by others and was only trying to do the right thing. Maybe I need to give myself more credit.

A fluttering sound pulls me from my thoughts. It's followed by a bird's sweet chirp. The melody echoes through the grand hallway, suggesting that the bird is stuck in here and not outside. I decide to find it, following the sounds. I'm still lost, but maybe I can at least save this bird. Even better, maybe this bird will show me a way out of here that's not guarded.

It sings, welcoming the morning, and I follow until I catch sight of the tiny thing and smile. It's barely larger than my thumb, with blue and green feathers. It sits perched on the arm of a chair, shiny black eyes blinking as I approach. But I get too close and it flies away, further down the hall. I continue to follow it until I hear a little thump and find it sitting on a windowsill.

It hops on one leg, feathers spread around it in a little arc. It's injured, must have tried to fly through the window even though it's tinted.

"Oh no," I whisper to the bird, "don't be scared. I'm going to help you get out of here."

This time it has no choice but to let me approach, and I push on the window. It doesn't give. It's bolted to the frame. I look down at my dress, trying to figure out how to use the material to safely pick up a bird. I don't want to touch it with my bare hands in case it's diseased.

A hand appears, snatching the bird so fast that I jump.

Brisa's hand.

"You snuck up on me," I gasp. I hurry to curtsy, hoping I'm doing this right.

"I have a tendency to do that." She holds the bird in her palm and pets its tiny head with her dainty finger. "They get in here sometimes when we leave the doors open at night," she says, smiling at the bird. "Tell me, Evangeline. Should I let it go free?"

This feels like a trick question. I swallow hard. "It's a bird. It's not meant to live indoors."

"Oh no? What about in a beautiful bird cage? We have several throughout the palace. I could keep it as a pet."

"Maybe if it was raised in captivity, but it would be cruel to put a wild animal in a cage."

"Hmm." She nods. "But it's injured. Wouldn't it be cruel to let it go back out there where it will surely die?"

Would she rather I agree with her or speak my truth. I straighten, standing tall. "You don't know that for sure."

"I've been around long enough to know it's very likely." She raises an exposed shoulder. She's not dressed in the gown from the party anymore. She wears a silky cream nightgown, and I have to force myself to not think of Adrian in her bed. She commanded he go to her chambers, so it stands to reason sex had something to do with it.

"It's your choice," I say finally. "I trust you to know what's best."

Her smile quirks. "I wish I believed you." And then she squeezes the bird. It cries out with a mangled squawk and goes silent in her stone-like hand. I stare, horrified. She drops it to the ground like garbage, feathers bent and broken. "Sometimes," she says, "it's better to end a life than to allow it to suffer." She steps closer and runs fingers along my cheek; my stomach twists, revolted by the feathers stuck to them. "If you continue to live as a human, that's what your life will be. Pain and suffering. What we're offering you is a second life, a better life. Very few people get that offer."

"And I'm grateful," I whisper.

"We'll see," she replies, and then she floats away like a ghost in the night. She's levitating a few inches off the ground and I wonder if she was the one who taught Adrian how. Or maybe it's because she's his master? No wonder she was able to sneak up on me! I swallow hard and stare down at the dead bird. If it weren't for me, it might still be alive because I'm certain her actions weren't to put the bird out of its misery, it was to let me know how much power she has over me.

I hope she believes me--that she thinks I want this and she wants this, too.

But I don't and I never will.

I don't care if her offer of a second life is filled with all the riches in the world. And like that bird, she wants to put me in a pretty cage. I can't let it happen.

"There you are," Adrian calls to me as he strides down the hall. "You're not supposed to be in this wing of the palace. This is Brisa's wing."

I nod. "Yeah, I just found that out."

He frowns and stops when he notices the dead bird. He doesn't say anything, and neither do I. He takes my hand and leads me away.

"Sorry, I got lost after the party," I whisper. "Do you know Sebastian's here? He thinks I killed his brother."

Adrian gives me a look that says, *"Well, you did kill his brother,"* so I return with one that says, *"Yeah, but only because you forced me into the situation."* He rolls his eyes as if to say, *"My, you're so ungrateful."*

Or something like that.

It's not as if I can read his mind with only a look.

"Come on," he says suddenly, "we need to move." He picks me up, dress and all, and we're flying through the halls. It's only when I catch a glimpse of the sunrise outside a window that I realize why. He doesn't want to get stuck anywhere else in this building for the day. He wants to be stuck with me.

When we make it back to the room, he sets me down simply as if the levitating trick is a normal occurrence for him. I'm still a little stunned but I'm also really tired. I strip out of my dress, not even caring that Adrian has a full view of my undergarments. My mind is thick with oncoming sleep. Between the flight and the time change and staying up all night to party with scary vampires, I'm done. I keep my slip on because it's easier than finding pajamas, and crawl into the blankets, pulling pins from my hair and tossing them to the floor. I burrow down into the fluffy pillow and close my eyes. Adrian lays down beside me. I don't know what I was expecting him to do, but it wasn't that. Before I can read anything into it, sleep takes me away.

I dream of birds.

Beautiful little green and blue birds. They descend on me like a cloud of locusts, clawing at my face, drawing blood. Wings flutter all around me, a tornado of feathers and claws and beaks. I scream and swat them away, but they keep coming. More and more. I fall to my knees, and they start to peck--little knives stabbing me. Over and over. I continue to scream and fight, but it's no use. There are too many of them. Beautiful little monsters.

Something cold shakes me. "Angel," a voice says. "Wake up."

My eyes pop open, and I bolt upright. I'm covered in sweat, and my heart pounds. My eyes try to adjust in the darkness, searching for the birds.

"You're okay. It was a nightmare." Adrian's voice reaches through the panic like water to a flame. He pulls me into his lap and rubs my back, shushing me. As sleep lifts, I find myself leaning into him.

This is not good.

This is so good. This is--

I scurry away and jump off the bed. "I'm okay now. Sorry." I run my hands through my hair. They're still shaking.

"You don't have to apologize to me." His voice drifts through the darkness. I can barely etch out his figure, but he's still sitting on the bed. "I used to have night-mares, too. There's no shame in it."

"What did you do to make them go away?"

"I became the nightmare."

CHAPTER 24

Sometime later I fall back asleep, and then the day repeats itself. And it happens again, and again, and again. I spend daylight hours sleeping off the nightly parties that Brisa requires us all to attend. Each seems to grow more wild than the next. We dress in the attire of courtesans to dance and mingle. It's mostly vampires, but there are a few humans as well. There's always food and drinks for us and endless blood for them. They mix it with all types of alcohol, creating their own versions of champagne and wine and more options than I can count. The vampires don't seem to be affected by the alcohol all that much, but it creates different tastes and ways for them to enjoy the blood.

And still, I can't help but notice the way they look at me and the other humans. No amount of blood bags will compare to drinking straight from our veins. They want us. We're the temptation they're not allowed to have.

Not only are they forbidden from feeding on humans, but the bloodline from Brisa makes it harder for them to break her commands. However, I know from experience that there are ways around it. Vampires can drink when they intend to turn us, they can drink if they're instructed to kill us, and they can push past Brisa's commands when they're so young that the bloodlust takes over.

I don't let myself forget that, given the chance, every last one of them would eat me alive. Adrian doesn't either. He stays close to my side at all times unless Brisa orders him away. When she does, I force myself not to think of what they might be doing. I don't walk back to my room alone again and Adrian never gives me a key. Night after night I wait for him to come for me and he always turns up right before dawn. Even though I hate it, I learned the first time that it's better to stay where the crowds are, especially since Sebastian always seems to be around. He doesn't talk to me anymore, but he watches, and he listens. He's building his case against me, I'm sure of it. He wants me to pay for Hugo's death with my life.

Adrian and I are still staying in the same room, but he doesn't show affection for me in private like he does for the court. I prefer it that way. When I sleep, he usually works from a laptop. After a week here he convinced Brisa to allow him a computer with internet connection so that he can continue to do business with his coven back home, but he keeps the laptop locked up in a safe whenever he's not using it. She's expressly forbidden me from touching it, but I still keep waiting for the opportunity to get my hands on it, hoping I can get a message to my friends and family back home. It never happens. And so the cycle continues––parties and sleep.

"What are you always writing in there?" Adrian asks me one evening. I'm sitting on the bed with a tray of fruit for breakfast at my side and the notebook Remi gave me open in my lap.

"Not always writing," I say, "mostly I'm doodling. And I'm surprised you haven't spied on it."

"I have no interest in invading your privacy."

I snort. "Sure, keep telling yourself that."

I've been writing out some of my feelings but I'd never show anyone those. I'm mostly drawing pictures from home, which aren't quite as embarrassing. They're the things I want to commit to memory in case I never see them again. I tried to sketch Felix and Ayla and my mom, but they all turned out terrible. Eventually, I'll get my hands on some electronics and can cyber stalk their lives from afar.

I moved on to objects, and lately I've been trying to get the feather talisman right. I know it's only a symbol of feathers crossing with the little hook on the bottom of one, but I can't seem to get it exactly right. I like what that woman said it represents: protection. I could use some of that right about now.

I decide to go out on a limb and flip the notebook

around so Adrian can get a look at it. He's sitting on the loveseat with his laptop in his lap, typing away. Apparently he already forgot that he cared about what I was doing with this notebook because he doesn't even look up.

"Whatever," I say, and flip it back around.

"You should be careful who sees that," he speaks up. So he did see it.

"Why?"

He lifts a shoulder. "Because it's not what you think it is."

"So what is it?"

"You ask too many questions."

"You started it."

He closes his laptop and sighs. "It's to do with those energy demons as you like to call them. That's all I can say but it should be enough."

As I suspected.

I close the book and take it with me to get ready that night. Remi is my only friend here and I don't get a lot of time with her. I want to ask her about the symbol, see if she knows anything more about it. When it's time to go to the dressing room, I do just that.

"I see you brought your notebook." She beams. "I'm so happy you're using it."

"Every day. This is saving my sanity. I can't thank you enough for giving it to me."

"It's my pleasure."

I hand it over to her. Despite it containing my

deepest thoughts and loads of bad sketches, I hope this step will help me in some small way. "Take a look."

She's been busy pinning my hair up, but she stops to take it. Half my hair hangs around my face and the other half is artfully swirled on top of my head.

She flips through it, stopping at a few of the journal entries, eyes roaming the words.

"They're really bad. So are the drawings," I interject. "But that's okay, I like it anyway. Keeps my mind busy and helps me process everything I'm going through."

She makes it to the pages I've been waiting for––the talisman images––and immediately hands the sketch-book back to me. "Turn to the right for me, please."

"Wait." I flash the pages at her. "Do you know anything about this symbol? Have you seen it before?"

Her face is impossibly blank as she studies it for a minute. "I don't. Sorry, Eva."

There's something different about her tone, something fearful, and I know she's lying. I want to question her more, but she insists she doesn't have any answers for me, so I eventually put the notebook away. When it's time to move onto my makeup and wardrobe, she says she has a headache and leaves me with the other servants. What is Remi hiding?

She doesn't show up to dress me the next night.

It's almost a month into my stay here that I wake up in the middle of the day, sitting upright with all sleepiness gone. My internal time clock has completely flipped from day to night. Since Brisa keeps me busy with her parties, I always end up sleeping the day away.

Not this time.

I blink the haze away and look for Adrian. He's not here. I've been waiting for this to happen. The idea came to me after that night I accidentally stumbled into Brisa's wing of the palace and Adrian swooped me up and flew us back to our room before I could blink twice. Fact is, this palace isn't completely ready for vamps, and that means there are places I can go to during the day that they cannot.

Still in my pajamas, I go to the door and peer out into the hallway. It's empty. This part of the palace is safe for vampires and I know they get up to stuff during the daylight hours, but I stay far away from whatever it is they're doing. I'm almost afraid to find out.

But someone is responsible for the deaths of all those princes. My first thought is Tate, but now that I've met Brisa, I can understand why she'd have many more enemies and some in her own court. I don't know what I'm looking for exactly, but I brave the hallway and hurry in the direction I committed to memory. I hope Brisa hasn't outfitted her entire wing with UV resistant windows yet, or I'm screwed.

"Fiona, are you hungry, my love? What are you doing awake?" I jump into an alcove when I hear Sebestian's voice up ahead.

"Bad dream. I wanted to find you." Her voice is sultry and welcoming, but he doesn't take the bait.

"You know the rules. Go back to the room. You can't be out during daylight hours."

So it's not just me. Maybe all the humans are relegated to our rooms during the day. There was a night during one of the parties that I tried to "wander" off and guards stopped me from getting very far. They seemed pretty angry with me then. I don't think I could get away with it twice.

I hold my breath when Sebastian and Fiona walk past. He's got his hand wrapped tight around her wrist and whispers harshly in her ear. I don't know what he's saying, but she's in trouble.

Maybe she's like me. Maybe she's here because she has to be, not because she wants to be. I never thought about that, I always assumed the other humans were traitors to their own kind. Could it be possible that I'm not the only one here pretending?

When they're gone, I'm faced with two choices. Keep exploring and risk discovery, or go back to safety. Me being me, I keep going.

A couple minutes later and I'm in Brisa's wing. It's quiet and sunlight streams through the windows, golden light that brings tears to my eyes. I didn't realize how much I missed it. I want to go to it, to soak in it and close my eyes, but I know I can't.

What am I even looking for? I don't know. Something. There's got to be something, some kind of clue.

That's when I see two human maidservants walking by. If anyone knows about the secrets of this place, it would be them, right?

"Excuse me?" I wave them down. "I'm wondering if you could help me with something?"

They look at me like deers in headlights. One points and starts yelling, "Guards!"

I guess that's my cue to leave.

Vampire guards aren't like regular guards. They're so much faster. A human wouldn't have a chance against them, so it's a dang good thing I'm not like other humans around here. I channel the venom and take off at incredible speed, rounding the hallway corners and diving back into the room before they can catch me.

I'm gasping for breath when I look up to see Adrian. He stands towering above me, his hands in fists at his sides.

"I know," I gasp out. "You don't have to lecture me."

"If you break Brisa's rules and they find you out there, they will kill you."

"How unfair is it that I'm here of all places and I can't even explore?"

"Is that what you were doing? Don't lie to me."

I shrug. "I was hoping to figure out whoever's been killing the princes. In case you forgot, that includes you." I point. "Someone wants you dead."

"A lot of people want me dead," he replies. "I'm used to it. Now get back to bed."

I roll my eyes but do as he says, adrenaline making it

impossible to fall asleep. I wish I did, because it's that very night, at one of Brisa's monotonous parties, that everything changes.

The French people don't typically celebrate Halloween, but Brisa announces that we're going to anyway--with a masked ball. I can't believe it's still October and that we're not well into November by now. Time has started to draw in on itself and I don't like that--I feel disoriented and want to demand to look at a calendar. But I don't demand anything. I can't. Not here.

True to Brisa's tastes, we're required to wear historical outfits. I don't get to choose what I wear. Ever. The servants always take care of that, and I never complain to them since none of this is their fault. I'm assuming Brisa is choosing my outfits, like a little girl playing with her dollies. Of course, I'm not the only doll, I'm one of at least a hundred. And all of us have painted smiles on our faces because we know the alternative could mean death.

Tonight, they dress me in a bright white gown. It's looser than the others and doesn't require a corset underneath--finally! I smile as the fabric sparkles under the candlelight.

"Wow," I whisper, appraising myself in the mirror. "This is my favorite one yet."

"Just wait," Remi says conspiratorially. "We're not done."

I hate that she's the only human servant here who I

suspect isn't under a compulsion. The woman simply has too much fiery life left inside her. I hope she leaves this place one day and never returns. I can see her hatred of Brisa in her hazel eyes and hear it in her careful voice when we talk about the queen, even if she does her best to keep it hidden. She produces a set of sheer angelic wings and fastens them to the back of the gown. Then she paints gold shimmery dust all over my neck and on the bridges of my cheekbones. My hair is braided intricately down my back with little gold gems twisted throughout. Lastly, she ties a gold Venetian mask over my smoky eyes. I stare at myself in the mirror because I don't think I've ever looked more beautiful.

"Good luck tonight." She hugs me, whispering in my ear. "Keep your eyes open."

She leaves me in the dressing room before I can question her, the others scurrying after her. I watch closely as they go, looking for the auras as I often do. They're dim, but they're always there when I make an effort to see them. I hope that means one day they can be saved from the compulsions. I squint to get a better look. Does Remi have one? For a moment, I think maybe she doesn't. She turns back and winks at me, and then closes the door.

I gape after her, wide awake despite my lack of sleep. Is Remi one of the energy demons? But she's so kind, so helpful. How did she get in here? Is she planning to help me? Hurt me?

I start toward the door to follow after her, but it opens into me, nearly knocking me over. I stumble back and then Adrian is there, catching me. He steadies my body, and I gaze up at him, momentarily mesmerized. He's dressed completely in black, from the doublet vest and fine tunic, down to the breeches, tights, and boots. He's grumbled over the clothing here enough times that I know he hates everything about them, but I've grown to like him this way––my dark prince. His mask matches mine, elegant shape, but is matte black. And at the top of his head, resting in his curls, are two crimson horns.

"So, your true self is revealed," I tease.

He smirks and sets me upright. My body burns in each place he touches.

"I thought it would only be fitting if we went as a matching set."

So he picked this dress for me. My cheeks warm at the realization. "The devil and an angel?" I raise an eyebrow. "Aren't they supposed to be enemies?"

"That's what makes it interesting." He takes my hand and leads me to the ballroom as he's done so many times before. But there's something about tonight that feels different. I'm unsettled, trying to figure it out. Is this the night the vampires turn me? Is it when hunters come to save me? Or are the demon-things here on some sort of mission?

I can't figure it out, but I'm certain there's something going on. Like a change in the weather, it can be subtle at first and then one day a new season blankets the world. It's happening.

I squeeze his hand. "You promise you'd help me, remember?" I whisper. We haven't spoken of it again since arriving, not since he took me out into the garden and demanded I keep my mouth shut. When he takes me to the catacombs to turn me, I will be saved the next day, pulled from the grave before I can turn. I'll be free to run away. It's not the life I would choose but it's better than becoming a permanent fixture in this court. I'm still not sure what will happen after that, but with Adrian's venom also in my human veins, I'm hoping it will be enough to keep me one step ahead of Brisa.

He squeezes my hand back and nods once.

I know I shouldn't, I know it's completely foolish, that he's tricked me time and again, but I think this time he's being honest.

"I trust you," I say. "Please don't hurt me again."

He stops abruptly, turns, and stares into my eyes. There is nobody else in the hall save for a few guards down at the far end. He doesn't speak or frown or smile. Nothing. His expression is unreadable, eyes hooded in shadows behind his Venetian mask as he takes me in. I'm certain he wants to say something, but the moment passes without a word. My heart skitters for reasons I can't name.

CHAPTER 25

The ballroom is decorated in a gothic style with dark red roses and black candles dripping long rivers of wax. Gauzy black fabric has been draped across the ceiling so that only the center crystal chandelier hangs down. The candles burn softly, the shrouded light creating an air of mystery to the event. It's perfect for Halloween, but I'm not sure I'll be able to enjoy myself tonight. I'm way too nervous. Adrian runs a thumb along the edge of my wrists, as if he can sense my emotions and wants me to relax. Trepidation is probably written all over my face despite the mask.

We mingle with the other guests for a few minutes, and I turn on my charm as best I can despite the nerves.

"You look lovely tonight, Evangeline," Katerina says. She's on Magnus's arm and they're also a matching set--dressed in peacock colors with feathered masks.

They've warmed up to me a little in my time here, but I still think they'd rather it be Kelly on Adrian's arm tonight. They begin to talk with Adrian and my mind wanders.

"Did you hear? There are only three princes left," someone whispers behind me. I make a point to listen.

"I heard that it was a rumor. Are you sure?"

"I'm sure. Someone's been killing them off. That's why Brisa brought all her courtesans here. The princes, too, of course."

"To protect us or investigate us?"

"Both."

I never turn around to see who's talking. I don't need to. If it's gossip among the courtesans then everyone will know. I'd foolishly assumed they already did—— Adrian did. I wonder if this will change things. I imagined myself to be a bit of a detective when I arrived here, thinking I'd uncover things of my own, but that proved impossible. Is Sebastian creepy as heck and possibly the killer? Sure. But it could be Tate and whatever organization he's with, or it could be Magnus and Katerina. Or anyone else for that matter. What worries me the most is eventually he or she or they will get to Adrian. I won't survive without him.

Eventually, the crowd separates and quiets as Brisa sweeps into the room. She's ruthlessly beautiful in an emerald colored gown that's cut low to show off her supple curves, but that's not what's so eye-catching about her costume. A long green snake is wrapped over her shoulders and around her arms. It curls into its master, body slithering as it inspects us with beady eyes. My stomach clenches when she walks toward us, and I instinctively step back. Snakes are so not my thing.

"A devil and an angel," Brisa greets us with a coy smile. "How fitting."

"And let me guess, Medusa?" Adrian bows.

"Well, I couldn't fasten snakes to my hair, so I decided this would have to do." She winks playfully. "But you'd better stay back, Evangeline. The snake is venomous and deadly to humans."

My stomach coils. Her pet eyes me like I'm either a threat or a treat, and I take another step back. "At least your eyes can't turn me to stone," I joke shakily.

She grins. "Don't be so certain that I'm not a gorgon and a vampire."

It's a good thing gorgons are a myth because if she were both, she'd be unstoppable. She's already unstoppable. She ends the conversation by walking away, going to the front of the room, and clears her throat to speak. The chatter dies off as the guests take notice. Everyone turns to their queen.

"Welcome, my lovelies. I'd like to make a toast," she purrs and opens her arms wide.

The human servants enter at once, streaming through us in a line with trays of champagne flutes and hors d'oeuvres for the humans. Aside from a few regular glasses for the fledglings, the drinks are dark red from the blood mixed in. We take the drinks, and I grimace at the outfits the waitstaff are wearing. They're dressed in black overcoats with plague doctor masks, the creepy bird beaks strapped over their mouths and noses. Their wide brimmed hats cast shadows over their eyes, making it hard to distinguish any identifying features. I thank the man who serves me a drink, but he doesn't respond. I sigh and take a tentative sip. The carbonation burns my throat as it goes down.

"As many of you know by now, someone is after me." Brisa's voice sharpens. "So let's toast to the demise of my enemies, especially the pretenders of my own court."

She raises her glass, and we do the same, some with more enthusiasm than others. She's just watered the distrust among us. The seeds were planted long ago, but tonight, things have shifted in a matter of a few words. There are only three princes left and by now everyone must know. The rest of the vampires here have other titles modeled after the French courts of old, but they're not tied so closely to Brisa as Adrian, Sebastian, and Magnus. As a human, I'm nothing, and I'm okay with that. Except for Sebastian's, not a lot of eyes have been on me during my time here. They see me as Adrian's newest accessory and nothing more.

"Now, have fun," she coos, "or I'll think you don't like me."

The orchestra strikes up, and people move into

formation, some on the dance floor, others to the edges of the room to mingle. It may be dressed differently, but it's like every other night, and I'm weary. I don't want to party. I don't want to gossip. I don't want to pretend that I'm happy here for another moment. It's been weeks, and nothing has happened. We're all stuck here in an endless loop, like snowflakes being tossed about in a snowglobe.

"Come on," Adrian whispers, taking my hand. "You know what to do."

And it's true. I've learned the dances by now. We begin the group waltz, and the champagne settles in my blood, making me feel lighter. I'm passed from Adrian, to other vampires, and even another human fledgling. It's a little more fun than some of the other dances, and I try to enjoy myself. But the music gathers speed. This hasn't happened before. Faster and faster, until I'm being tossed about like a ragdoll. Someone brushes up against my wings and they tug on my shoulder blade.

I cry out as Sebastian pulls me into his steel-like arms. He's dressed in gray and wearing a wolf mask that covers the left side of his handsome face. "Let me help you," he says roughly, then he dances with me so fast that my feet catch and I trip over the hem of my dress. He picks me up *after* I hit the marble floor. "Sometimes I forget how klutzy humans can be." He laughs as if this is all a game.

"Your costume is perfect, by the way," I bite back. My knees ache, and I long to sit down. I look around for

Adrian, but his back is to me as he dances with another woman. "Adr--"

Sebastian's hand clasps over my mouth as he continues to dance with me. Round and round we go. My hands itch for a stake so I can end him, but I haven't touched a stake since I left New Orleans. "Don't think such awful things." He laughs in my face. "You claim to want to be a part of this court, don't you? Adrian's little angel."

My eyes go wide. Does he know what I'm thinking? Since he's a prince, he's got to be old. Adrian told me Brisa made all her princes centuries ago and hasn't turned anyone else since. She surrounded herself with men she could trust. It was a strategic move on her part not to make any vampire princesses. She didn't want anyone who could compete with her beauty. What does she think of the female vampires in her bloodlines? What does she think of me?

"That's enough." Adrian appears beside us, and we blessedly stop dancing. The other dancers have no trouble continuing around us. Adrian's mouth is drawn into a thin line as he glares at Sebastian, anger radiating from him. "I'll take my date back now."

Sebastian releases me easily, as if this were all a fun joke. "You really are a bore sometimes, Adrianos. All that Greek study did you no good if you ask me."

"Nobody asked you," Adrian bites back.

Greek study? I'm keenly interested in Adrian's past but after his confessions of killing his wife and unborn child, I haven't asked him anything. From what I learned in school, the ancient Greek people were really into philosophy and arts, so it must have something to do with that. Maybe one day he'll tell me all about his life before immortality.

"If you care about her so much, why aren't you more affectionate with her?" Sebastian questions. "Maybe Evangeline wants to dance with other men."

"I don't," I'm quick to say.

Adrian continues to glare. "I have nothing to prove to you."

"Don't you?" Sebastian's mocking tone dissolves into one of accusation. "Because everyone is wondering what's going on with you, Adrian. You rarely take on any prodigies and you recently lost your only child."

"Don't talk about Kelly!" Adrian roars.

"And now, you're here with this new girl, and you're dragging your feet. Turn her already. You can turn her at any moment. Brisa told me she gave you permission the first night you arrived. So what are you waiting for?"

I blink at them, my chest tightening. Adrian's been protecting me, but in doing so he's also keeping me here in an endless loop. If he'd go through with our plan, I could be free by now.

"Oh, she doesn't know . . ." Sebastian laughs. "Well, it sounds like you have some explaining to do, brother." He pats Adrian on the shoulder and then strides away, taking another human dance partner. He whispers into her ear, and she laughs, her cheeks becoming pink. I turn back to Adrian and blink up at him.

"Is this true?"

He doesn't say anything, which says everything I need to know. I turn and stride away.

CHAPTER 26

I'm done with this party. I wish I could be done with him and this palace and the stupid little room we share. I wish I'd never walked into that casino. I wish I'd never met Adrian. I wish none of this had ever happened.

I run back to the room, attempting to slam the door behind me, but Adrain catches it. "You have to go back to the party," he hisses to my back. "Brisa wants us all to be there."

His voice aches like it's painful for him to disobey her. I know it is. And yet, he's here. I wonder what kind of order she gave. Was it a command or a request?

"I'm risking everything to follow you here," he goes on, "don't you see that I care for you?"

I turn to face him. "All I see is a liar in a mask."

He rips his mask off and tosses it to the floor. "I shouldn't be in here, but I am, with *you*."

"Tell me why."

He grabs my hand and tugs, shaking his head. "It doesn't matter right now. We have to go back."

"Leave me alone! I'm not under Brisa's or your command," I growl. "You can't make me do a damn thing."

"Why do you have to be such a pain in the ass?" He changes direction, stalking toward me.

"It takes one to know one."

He pushes me up against the edge of the four-poster bed. My back presses into the pillar of wood, but I hardly notice it because every part of me lights up. The venom in my blood sparks to life, and I can feel, see, and sense everything. And it's all directed toward Adrian like he's the storm on the horizon. The electricity between us is unmistakable. It draws my breath from my body, and I try to look away.

"Look at me," he whispers. He takes my face into his cold hand and turns me to face him. His fingers wrap around my jaw, featherlight. His thumb tilts my head upward to look at him. "What is it about you that draws me to you?"

My lips part, but I don't know what to say. It's the same for me, and I hate and love it equally. It's an enjoyable pain, and I'm sick for liking it.

"My winning personality and kickass combat skills?" I respond. "Or maybe it's my wit. Or maybe it's because I'm an innocent little virginal angel. I know how you like my blood."

"You're insufferable." His blue eyes wrinkle at the sides, anger dissipating.

"Don't do that." I press my hands to his chest and try to push him back. He doesn't move. It's like pushing into a stone statue.

"Don't do what?"

"Flirt with me," I growl. "Play with my heart. Lead me on. Lie to me. Hurt me."

I don't know what I expect him to do. Apologize? Pout? Weave more lies? He does none of those things.

"I don't take orders from you," he says, eyes darkening.

"So what will you do, huh?" My hands press into his chest again. "Go back to your little party?"

"Brisa can wait." His voice is clipped.

"Like how you waited to let me go free?"

He grabs my wrists, wrenching my hands away and pushing me back against the post even harder. He holds my arms above my head and inches close, like a predator about to pounce on his prey. His body comes closer still, until it's flush against mine, until I can feel every muscle. I can sense something in him fighting off Brisa's instructions to enjoy the party. He should be there, but he wants to be here, and that changes things.

My body betrays me, longing pooling low in my stomach. Everything buzzes––my skin is alive with his presence. His cedar and bergamot scent wraps around me, and I breathe him in. He shifts his hands so that he's only got one holding my arms above my head. This time, I don't fight him. His other hand trails down my arm, fingertips feathering around my shoulder, up my neck, and around the back of my head. I shiver as he unties my mask. The second it falls to the floor and his fingers claw into my hair, I forget everything.

I know what's happening. None of this takes me by surprise, not as it should. Not even for a second. The moment his lips claim mine, I finally admit that I've been waiting for this moment for months.

It's inevitable.

And wrong.

And so, so right.

The kiss is not tender. It's demanding and claiming and exploring.

We move right for the bed, and things progress quickly. I let it. I want it. We continue on a brazen path until it's time to lose my virginity. Not only will it keep me safer around the other vampires, but I'm tired of waiting for this to happen. *I need it.* My mind is ready. My body is pleading. And my heart is wanting-- wanting this to work, wanting it to be real, for him to feel everything I'm feeling right now.

And I'm scared as hell.

But not for the reasons I thought I would be. The physical act itself is inevitable. I'm a grown woman, and this is a natural part of growing up. No, that's not what scares me. It's everything else, it's what will change between us, it's my own emotions, and especially his. I'm foolishly opening myself to be vulnerable with someone who could ruin me with his coldness. He can have me and just as easily destroy me. But despite all that, I still want this with him.

My hands tug at his layers of clothing, eager to get the last of them off. When there's nothing between his body and mine, he stops for a moment, staring down at me. He's frozen, and I don't know how he does it because I'm burning up. Something unreadable flashes in his eyes, and then it's gone as quick as a falling star. "Are you sure?" he asks, searching my face.

I laugh. "You're the one who said I needed to take care of it."

He growls a little. "I'm sorry for that. I was thinking of your safety among my coven and not your feelings as a human woman."

I nuzzle into him, kissing along his collarbone. I speak between kisses. "Wow, I never thought I'd see the day that Adrianos Teresi would apologize."

"Don't get used to it." He laughs back and then descends on me, kissing down my collarbone this time.

It sends another bolt of electricity down my spine, and I arch into him, ready for more. "Yes, this is what I want."

His kisses continue for long agonizing minutes, some gentle and others not. Emotions flood my body, and I don't know if my heart can take another second. I try to cloud them over, to focus on the physical motions only, but my feelings for Adrian shine through with the force of the sun. There's nothing I can do to stop my falling for him, not falling--*jumping*. I'm doing this to myself. He may have gotten me here, but this moment is my choice and one I'd choose a thousand times over. When I told him I wanted this, I meant it. To not have this moment would hurt too much, would rip me open and leave me for dead.

Adrian takes his time, and it's evident he's done this countless times before. Maybe I'm like every other woman who's been in his bed, but I tell myself that can't be true. I break away for a moment to gaze at him. I want to see into his eyes, hoping I'll find something real there. An answer to a question I've been asking my whole life. Why does he have to be the most beautiful man I've ever seen? As evil as she is, I can't blame Brisa for picking him because anyone would want him. His blue eyes are hooded with desire, as if it's killing him to hold back, as if this is tormenting him as much as it is me.

"The power you hold over me," he whispers low, "it's . . . " His voice trails off. He doesn't have a word for it. It's perhaps the most relatable thing he's ever said, and he didn't actually say anything.

"I know." I smile and laugh, that power filling me up like a woman possessed. "You don't have to explain it to me. I know."

Because I feel the exact same way.

We kiss again, and then we're doing more than kissing.

It's surreal, but it's also the realest moment of my life.

As he takes me, I simultaneously want it to end and to last forever. It would be easier if he treated this like a transaction, like another one of his deals. But he worships my body, bringing it to life in a way I never knew was possible. No other man could make me feel this good. Nobody. My emotions build at the same time my thoughts melt away, until everything is taken over by pure sensation, like ocean waves crashing into the shore.

He holds me as those sensations begin to ebb away, whispering into my ear in a language I don't know. He runs his nose down my jaw and to my neck, kissing there as he speaks. His breath tickles, and goosebumps dance over my skin. His cool hands freely roam over me until I can't take it. I turn so our legs are entwined and press into him.

"Are you okay?" he asks. I gaze up, noticing his fangs have appeared. I'm not afraid. In fact, I'm overcome with something I never expected––a need for my lover to bite me.

"Yes," I whisper, followed by a whispered, "please."

He whips away with a groan.

He can't. I know that. It might even be impossible without Brisa's permission, might be too much for him to fight this time. And it's stupid to want it. Dangerous. Foolish. But I remember that euphoric feeling when Hugo bit me, and I can only imagine what it will be like with Adrian, especially with my senses so alive as they are. Allowing him to feed on me may even trump what we just did, as impossible as that seems.

He manages to get his fangs to retract, and then he's kissing me again. It's as tender as a lover's confession, and I'm paralyzed by it. Am I already in love? Has it already happened? Is he in love?

No he's not, and I'm not, but . . .

Someone pounds on the door.

Adrian pauses only long enough to yell, "Go away." It doesn't work. Whoever's at the door keeps knocking. With a frustrated sigh, he peels himself away and slides into his leggings. He pads over to open the door, peeking his head through.

"This had better be important," he hisses at whatever unfortunate soul has interrupted us.

"Brisa has commanded everyone to join her outside for a special surprise," someone says apologetically. He sounds like one of the male servants.

"We'll pass," Adrian growls.

"You can't," the voice continues, "she specifically asked to make sure you and Eva are there. She's agitated that you left her party."

There's a long pause, but I already know this moment is over. "We'll be there." Adrian closes the door and turns on me with a regretful expression. "Get dressed, my angel. We have to go."

CHAPTER 27

One thing the palace of Versailles isn't lacking is gardens. They're the kind of impressive that's hard to comprehend in real life. I haven't been allowed out to explore them during the day, but at night Adrian and I have ventured into their sweeping grandeur during a few of the parties. I'm sure it's not the same experience without the sun, but I've let Adrian become my sun without realizing it. Maybe that was stupid, maybe it was a mistake, but it was also inevitable.

The gardens stretch around the palace for two thousand acres. Adrian says they're twice the size of Central Park. I've never been to Central Park, nor do I want to. Rumor has it New York City is rampant with vampires, far more so than New Orleans. All the best cities have a vampire infestation at this point. Any travel bug I would've had has been ruined by them. Truthfully, I'd love to see the world, and being in Paris without really being in Paris hurts my soul. But after this experience, the only places I'd feel comfortable traveling to are tiny boring towns without enough humans to keep vampires satisfied. But the suckers have even popped up in Hawaii and on most of the Caribbean islands, which aren't even all that populated. I don't know how the people stayed; I wouldn't want to be stuck with vampires on a little plot of land surrounded by a vast ocean.

This palace sort of feels like an island most days-- these gardens are my ocean. And instead of sharks to watch out for, I've got vampire guards with big guns and a queen I still can't figure out. Some days I think she hates me, others I think she likes me, and most days I don't think she cares one way or the other.

Adrian and I walk down the hallway hand in hand and my romantic heart leaps. I'm still so mixed up. I know how I feel about him, know that I want him, but I'm still aware of how messed up that is. He's the enemy, they all are, and I'm toeing a very dangerous line.

When we stride outside, the guests are gathered around the ballroom terrace. The thin crescent moon hangs high, and darkness covers the landscape. Brisa stands on a little podium, a grassy lawn stretching behind her. She's already started a speech, and Adrian and I sneak into the back of the onlookers. He squeezes my hand tighter. "Come on," he whispers, "let's go up front."

I'd rather not be here at all, let alone to go up front, but Adrian's already weaving through the crowd and tugging me along after him. Maybe he wants to make sure Brisa sees us so she isn't angry that we ditched her party. Awareness needles my cheeks as I realize these vampires can probably tell what Adrian and I did. They wouldn't know except that the scent of my blood would have changed with the loss of my virginity. But it's not like these vamps aren't enjoying themselves whenever and wherever they wish. Why should I care? I hold my head up high and smirk at anyone who gives me a knowing glance or a sly smile. There's no reason to be ashamed. Besides, the whole vampires loving virgin blood thing is creepy and their problem, not mine.

Brisa falters when she sees us, her voice slipping for the slightest moment. She blinks it away and returns to her speech. "There's a reason I called you all here," she says. "You're my closest friends and family, and I wanted you in my presence again. You've all been living at my new court for at least a month now. Have you enjoyed yourselves?"

People cheer and nod along, but the enthusiasm is a bit mixed. Like Adrian, so many of these vampires are eager to get back to their covens and manage their work. Time may be arbitrary to Brisa, but it's not to the many businesses and humans outside of the palace. Brisa's gaze surveys the crowd, appraising us like jewels in her collection, some of us more shiny and valuable than others.

"I have news." She motions for someone in the crowd to join her. When Sebastian climbs onto the podium next to her, my stomach hardens. "Go ahead, tell them what you know," her voice goes sharp, "tell no lies."

It's a command.

If he tells no lies, will he have to out himself as being the killer? I've wondered if he's the one who's been responsible, acting like he was on Brisa's errand when really he was working against her. I have no real proof, just a thought that led to another and another until I started to become convinced. When Kelly died, Cameron had targeted Adrian, and I've wondered if he was in part compelled, because any hunter in their right mind wouldn't have tried that alone.

I've kept this to myself, but now I suddenly wish I'd told Adrian my suspicions.

Sebastian speaks as if he knows everything. "I've rooted out the person responsible for going after the princes. The traitor has been successful in killing all but two of us." Two? What about Magnus? "That's right, unfortunately earlier tonight during the party Magnus faced true death."

"I felt his loss the moment he was taken from me," Brisa says angrily, her eyes watering. "And Sebastian witnessed it."

I squeeze Adrian's hand at the news. This can't be good. What if they're going to blame me for it? Adrian and I left the party early, something everyone who cares to know will know by now. And I can't forget Sebastian's many threats toward me. When his eyes land on me and he points right in my direction, I refuse to believe it. He's not really accusing me, is he? It's true about Hugo, but he doesn't know that for sure. And how could I possibly have killed princes who weren't even on the same continent as me?

"Katerina!" he calls out, voice cracking like a whip, and all hell breaks out.

I'm pushed to the ground, my knees hitting the stones first. Then Adrian is on top of me, protecting me with his body. The woman is directly behind us and screaming out obscenities between sobs. "You're a liar, Sebastian! I *loved* him."

But it's no use.

Guards detain her and nobody defends her. Adrian helps me up, and I rub my palms on my dress while trying to locate the woman. Her cries were anguished and I believed she loved her maker and partner even more than the rest of us are supposed to. What if she is innocent? I don't think it would matter. Brisa has already made up her mind.

Katerina is a beautiful woman, and possibly became a threat to Magnus's loyalty. If he had to choose between his lover and his maker, I genuinely believe he'd have chosen Katerina. And Brisa knew it too. At this point it doesn't matter, Brisa seems happy to be rid of the couple.

"Katerina wants to take out our monarchy, and I have proof," Sebastian continues, "She recently traveled to every location where the princes were murdered.

When I went to confront them, I caught her with the stake."

Katerina gapes at him. "I didn't see who killed him and neither did you. I only picked up the stake after he was gone. And I was doing my job when I traveled." Tears run down her cheeks, makeup smearing. "We both were."

"That's enough." Brisa flicks her wrist toward Katerina and the guards. "You know what to do."

So that's it? She's going to believe Sebastian just like that? He was commanded not to lie but Brisa never questioned his story. It's perfect––if he's the real killer, he now has a scapegoat and only one more person standing between him and Brisa. And that person is Adrian.

The guards drag Katerina out toward the gardens, which makes no sense to me. Wouldn't they put her in a dungeon? Kill her on the spot? What's out in the gardens? We stay in place, everyone silent on the terrace.

"Well, don't be so glum, this is a party!" Brisa opens her arms wide. "And I have another surprise for you in a few minutes, so don't go anywhere."

She turns away, eager to watch the gardens and see if she can spot what's happening to Kat. To please Brisa, we talk amongst ourselves. Some people here seem glad that Katerina is gone. Others . . . not so much. Their mouths are set and eyes are glum. Katerina was a favorite at court. Is this what happens to the female favorites around here?

I stick close to Adrian's side as we mingle through the crowd. I'm never letting him go again. Well, that's if Brisa doesn't command him to leave me. Since that first party, she's called him to her chambers on multiple occasions. We never talk about it. Now I suddenly want to talk about it and to demand he never entertain her again, but I don't.

"Come up front. Both of you," Brisa says, appearing at our sides. She slips a slim arm around my waist as well as Adrian's and directs us to the balcony at the head of the large terrace. I'm aware of the snake resting around her shoulders. It lays its little head on Adrian's arm and he pets it gently. I shiver, wishing that thing was long gone.

Brisa stands between us, a tiny woman with the power to ruin everything. I breathe slowly, filling my lungs with cool air, hoping to slow my heart. She needs to like me, to want me here, or I'm dead.

We lean on the railing and she whispers to the snake, "Go home now, Precious. You did good." It slithers down the steps.

"You can compel animals?"

"One of my many talents," she replies.

"She's the only vampire who can do it," Adrian adds. "The rest of us can compel adult humans and that's only if we're strong enough. Brisa is an incredible queen."

She waves the compliment off but I can tell she's

pleased. It's dark, but my eyes adjust thanks to Hugo's venom. I squint anyway, to be safe. She knows I was involved with hunters but she doesn't know about Hugo's venom. Standing this close to her kind of makes me want to throw up--I'm so nervous.

"What are we looking at?" I ask.

Brisa laughs and turns to Adrian. "Is she always this impatient?"

"Always."

"All humans are." Brisa smirks and pats me on the back. "It's okay. I was the same when I knew my time on this earth was so limited. You remind me a lot of myself, actually. Now tell me, are you glad you switched sides?"

I smile, putting on my best mask. I wish I still had the Venetian one covering my eyes but it's still back on the bedroom floor. I hope she can't see the worry on my face. "The hunters can't give me all this. Nobody can but you and Adrian can."

She nods. "He's been taking his time, hasn't he?"

It all comes back to me in a rush, the entire reason I was angry at Adrian in the first place. He could've put me in the catacombs weeks ago. My spine straightens and I'm not sure what to say. I don't want to make it sound like I don't want this. I do, but only so I can escape before the venom takes hold forever.

A woman's frantic screams roll across the gardens.

"Ah, that would be Katerina facing her mortality." And then the screams are swapped for thunderous booms. Fireworks light up the sky, glorious and sweeping through the darkness. The next ten minutes are filled with one of the most impressive shows I've ever seen, but I can't find it in myself to enjoy it. Not when I realize the truth--Katerina is dead, and those fireworks are what ended her. I'm not exactly sure how, but if I had to guess, I'd assume she was tied down to them. I always thought vampires had to be killed with a stake or the sun, but I guess there are more creative options. Blowing someone to pieces seems to do the trick. Or maybe my imagination is getting away with me and the guards simply used the noise of the show to muffle her death. Somehow, I doubt it.

The show ends, and I'm antsy to get back to the room and forget about this ever happening. Brisa smiles brightly and squeezes my shoulders. "Welcome to the family, Evangeline. It looks like our Adrian finally made you his tonight." She winks playfully, but there's an undercurrent of venom in her tone. "It's okay, I don't expect him to be celibate. Besides, you'll be one of us in three days anyway." I blink at her and then at Adrian. He smiles grimly and looks away. The corner of Brisa's mouth lifts. "Oh, didn't he tell you? Today was your last day as a human."

CHAPTER 28

I can't move. I'm numb. I glance at Adrian, pleading with my eyes for answers, but his are downcast, and his face is unreadable. Brisa grabs my hand and tugs me after her. Her grip is vise-like and far too strong, crushing my fingers without care. "We'd better get going before we run out of time," she says. Adrian follows behind us, and all I can hope is that his plan is still in motion. Did he ever find someone to get me out of there? Is he going to come back himself?

I knew this was coming, watched it coming, even. But no amount of knowing and waiting and watching could've prepared me for this moment. My heart slams against my chest like a drum, and I'm sure the vampires can hear it. Maybe that makes them more excited, maybe it's that beat that makes them the most hungry. And maybe I'm lucky that they're taking me to the catacombs and not feeding on me right here.

"And between you and me," she whispers, "I will let you feed directly on humans, and I'll even let you end some of their lives. It's cruel to keep new vampires from their base instincts but it's done for the betterment of our kind. You will get special privileges since you'll be a royal, but they have to stay a secret or the other vampires will get angry with me."

"What?" I balk at her. I wonder where they keep these humans. The palace is so big, they could be hidden anywhere. No wonder why I was forbidden from exploring! Plus, the vampires own property all over the world. It's almost comical that I thought she wasn't allowing this for her favorites, and surely for herself. I should've caught on before.

"I know, I'm nothing if not generous. We go for criminals and people who deserve to die. I have cultivated special relationships with prison wardens across the globe. They give me the ones who have no friends or family to ask after them." Brisa chuckles. "We're not complete savages. It's not like we're killing innocents anymore. We've learned, and we do better now."

Wait . . . my thoughts roll back to something she said before. "Royal?" I ask. That doesn't make sense. I'm going to be Adrian's prodigy, which would make me . . . what? What is the daughter of a prince? I don't know enough about this stuff to have the title off the top of my head, but I know it puts me far enough away from the crown that I'm not considered royal anymore. Or maybe it still does? I guess the royal family in England, the ones who are always all over the tabloids, call their grandchildren princes and princesses.

So maybe that's what she means. *Please let that be what she means . . .*

"What's Adrian's is mine," she answers.

This whole vampire family dynamic is twisted.

"Come, this way." The group moves around the edge of the palace toward the same area where Adrian and I were brought into a garage weeks ago. Everyone is laughing and cheerful, acting as if they didn't just witness one of their very own being brutally murdered. I'm having a hard time thinking or breathing, knowing that my life is about to end as well. I keep clenching and unclenching my fists, not sure what to do. How can I go along with this? I feel like I'm a kid marching up to the diving board for the first time, only this is one of the tall ones reserved for professionals. I don't know how I'm going to make it out alive!

I'm seriously praying that Adrian was honest when he said he was working on a way to get me out of those catacombs before my third day. Luckily, being down there should be better than trying to dig myself out of an actual grave. As we come around the corner of the palace, several of the human servants in the plague doctor costumes appear with more drinks to greet us on the driveway. The area is surrounded on three sides by the palace and one by a large golden fence. The stars twinkle above.

We raise our glasses. "A parting goodbye," Brisa says right before someone screams.

The plague doctor humans throw their trays at the vampires. They rip off their masks and drop their long coats, and time seems to stop. I recognize several of them; they are the hunters from New Orleans. My hunters--and my friends. But I don't have time to process much, because time speeds up again and the fight breaks out.

These hunters are prepared, with loads of stakes strapped on their bodies and crossbows in several of their hands. Adrian grabs me and pushes me back. "Stay here," he yells, and then he's flying out to meet the hunters. Stakes slice through the air, going right for him, but he dodges them all with practiced ease. He's so much faster than the rest of them.

There are far more humans than I've ever seen before. Somehow they have infiltrated the palace. Are they here because of me? I'm not sure how they figured out how to find me, but they must have. Part of me wants to go to them, and to be saved and rescued and to get far away from Brisa and Adrian and the rest of them. And another part of me wants to scream that they're here at all, because they're not going to survive this. I have seen for myself how cruel this court is--there will be no prisoners. It's dead or alive and that's it.

But they are here now, and if I can get away from Versailles, I would be stupid not to take my chance. I run toward them, hoping someone will give me a stake so I can fight at their sides. I catch sight of Seth and hurry to him. "Hey, what are you doing here?"

He gives me a hard look. "Get out of the way, you're not our target."

And then he's gone.

Okay, so maybe this isn't a rescue mission. But what the heck? Why did he talk to me like that? Am I just meant to stand back and watch?

And that's when I realize how much they are going after Adrian over anyone else. I would think they'd be going after the queen herself, but nope, everyone seems to have Adrian as their target. As the fight explodes into blood and chaos, vampires go down and so do humans. It's hard to watch, and I would give anything to join in.

Felix's face appears as the crowd surrounds me. He picks me up around the torso, dragging me to the edge of the fray. "We have to get you to safety," he mutters. "You should get out of here."

Once we're out of the craziness, I have to ask, "What are you guys doing here? Are you trying to kill Adrian?"

He sets me down abruptly and steps back. His eyes narrow into little slits and he stares at me as if he's seeing me for the first time. "Are you sleeping with him?"

I don't know how to answer that. My cheeks warm and I look away. It's all he needs to know. He takes another step back and lets out a small breath.

"We're here for Tate. Our target is your boyfriend. Funny, I thought I would save you in the process and we could go back to the way things were before you disappeared."

"I'm sorry," I whisper.

"Did you come here willingly? Just answer me that."

"Of course not."

His lips thin and he looks away, hands back on his stakes.

"Why do you want to kill Adrian? There are worse vampires here."

Those words turn his attention back to me and he glares. "You know what, Eva? Why don't you save yourself."

CHAPTER 29

*A*nd then as if I'm nothing to him, he's running back into the fight and my heart is breaking and it's all my own fault. He's right and he should hate me. I've become too soft, too trusting, when my heart should've stayed guarded. I dig my foot into the grass, because you know what? I thought Felix was my friend.

Another hunter comes barreling toward me, his eyes wide and his teeth bared. "You! This is all your fault!" He actually has the stake pointed at me, death in his eyes.

I ready my stance and channel my training. I'll fight him off if I need to. But I don't have to, because Adrian gets to him first, knocking him unconscious. He lands a foot away.

"Why does Tate hate you so much?" I demand.

"It's a long story."

"Where's Brisa?"

"Her guards already got her out of here. We need to get you to safety too."

"I don't think so," I say, my heart dropping as I point back to the drive. The tide has shifted and it has become painfully clear that the vampires are the stronger of the two groups here.

"Move out!" Felix calls, and the hunters take off, sprinting into the darkness.

But the remaining vampires are angry, and hungry, and they'll kill anyone they can. I can't let them kill my friends! I turn on Adrian. "Please don't let them kill them," I cry, "please, they don't know what they're doing. Tate set them up to this. They're not bad people."

Adrian shakes his head--and it sets me free. I'm done with him, with the lies, the manipulations, and the disappointments. I have to take matters into my own hands. I run toward the hunters, hoping to save whoever I can. Something metallic rattles through the air--a machine gun. Everyone drops to the ground, myself included, and my heart beats in my ears. Is that coming from the guards? Or from the hunters? Either way, this is it. We're all going to die right here at the foot of the palace.

The gunfire stops and I uncover my head to find a silver bullet embedded into the earth a mere two inches from my face. I remember what Tate said about silver bullets being used to slow the vampires down. My hope rises--does that mean my friends got away? It's hard to hope these things, when hope has been taken away from me so many times before. But when I look up, I find that most of the hunters are gone.

I don't see Seth or Felix.

I stand and wander through the bodies of what hunters didn't make it. When I see Kenton laying among the dead, my heart stops. His leg is twisted back behind him at an awkward angle and his eyes are wide open and staring into nothing.

No. No no no no no. This can't be happening.

I want to fall to my knees and sob, but Remi is at my side and pulling me away. "Don't feel sad," she says, "don't let anyone see you sad."

"What are you doing here?" I turn on her.

But she doesn't have an answer and I can't help but wonder if she had something to do with this attack. "What are you? Are you a human or not?" I ask her point-blank.

Her face shuts down and then she turns and runs away. I want to chase her down and demand answers but I can't seem to move with Kenton lying at my feet. The vampires will stred him to pieces before he even gets a chance to grow cold.

"Death is part of being a vampire." Brisa appears at my side. "You will get used to it. Come, I'm not going to let this deter us from our intentions for the night."

I blink at her as she leads me to a car, the first I've seen in a month, and we climb into the plush leather backseat. At least it's not one of the ones without windows. That other one felt like an early grave, but I guess that's fitting considering where I'm about to go. There are other cars waiting on the wide driveway as well, and other vampires that are left climb into those. I notice some of the other fledglings are along for the ride. Did everyone know about this night? Did they know this was their last day as a human, and Adrian decided not to let me in the loop?

I've always hated surprises . . .

Adrian climbs in, too, and I'm sandwiched between them in the back of the vehicle as we head toward Paris. Maybe I'm in shock, but I can't believe any of this is happening, or that the hunters just attacked and now we're back to business as usual minutes later.

Versailles is on the outskirts of the city, and I've been longing to go into the city itself since the moment the jet hit the runway. Maybe some of the people of the court have been allowed into Paris, I'm not sure, but Adrian and I have been ordered to stay put. It's one more thing I can add to my long list of resentments against Brisa.

As we drive through the beautiful historic city, it reminds me of New Orleans at night, and that reminds me of my friends. It's hard not to cry, but I don't let myself. Instead I focus on the view and keep pointing out the similarities of the cities to myself. It's not just in the architecture of some of the buildings, but in the small groups of people tittering down the sidewalks on their way home from the clubs and bars. Who cares if vampires are involved when the vices are served? It's a horribly brilliant exchange, and I'm sitting next to the mastermind.

Guilt wracks through me, because I put myself in this situation, because I was a fool. And now people are dead, my amazing, vibrant, funny, cute, awesome friend Kenton among them.

For a moment, I pretend that it's daylight, that we're on our way to enjoy the city like any other tourists. I try to imagine the last couple of hours as if nothing notable had ever happened. If I had my choice, we'd be going to the museums, to the top of the Eiffel Tower, to wander the treasure of the Louvre, and stop off at a bakery or a café to enjoy wonderful food and people-watch. If I could only be gifted a semblance of a normal life before . . . before . . . before . . .

We pull up to a church that I instantly recognize but whose name eludes me right now. My brain has gone fuzzy as the nerves have taken over. "If the humans would've allowed us to take over their landmarks sooner," Brisa says, "we would've never allowed a *fire* to destroy such a historic building." She says fire as if it's an avoidable nuisance and not a sad accident. "I've always loved Notre Dame, same is true of all the gothic architecture that is mostly gone now. France is my home. I've traveled the world, of course, but I always come back here. There's simply nowhere like France."

Notre Dame, that's right. Looking at it now is like coming to a church with a confession and being told I'm not forgiven. My eyes water again. I can't cry in front of her, and that makes it even harder.

The lights of the city twinkle on the inky black river. What's left of Notre Dame looms over us like a dark gothic mountain, gargoyles perched on its ledges. Through the haze of sadness, I recall what she's talking about, how years ago huge parts of this historic church caught on fire and burned to the ground. Investigators later said it was the fault of bad electrical wiring or maybe even a stray cigarette butt. Either way, it had been a tragedy that the whole world had watched from their television screens.

But do vampires really think that they could prevent something such as a fire? And what about an act of God? Could they stop a natural disaster like lightning from striking or a storm from raging? "You've seen it all, haven't you?" I ask numbly. "And you prefer the old ways to the new?"

"In some ways, yes." She smiles demurely. She's acting as if the hunter attack did nothing to ruin her good mood. What is wrong with this lady? "Do you know I've never made my own princess? I've only made sons and raised them to be powerful princes." I did know, but I don't say anything. She muses to herself as she continues. "Some say it's because I get jealous of women, but that's not really why, I just find that men are better company." I swallow, not sure what she means by that. Is she talking about sex? Should I take offense? Should I be grateful that I'm even in her presence right now? In the end, I decide it's best to keep quiet and let her continue. "Adrianos knows all about that. Don't you, Adrian?"

She's obviously talking about sex and it makes my stomach roll. For the first time since we climbed into this car, he makes eye contact with me. The pained look in his eyes does not bode well for me. "I do." Two words. That's all he says.

I look away.

We walk into the church with about thirty others following us. A lot of it is still roped off, but it doesn't matter. Brisa leads us to a staircase, and we immediately descend. "There are all sorts of entrances to the catacombs in Paris," she explains, "but I prefer this one. I like to keep things dramatic." She laughs at herself and most of the minions laugh along. She certainly does know how to put on a show.

It's too dark for humans to see, but I can. I don't say anything. I hold onto Adrian's rigid arm and act like I'm as blind as the rest of the humans. Someone lights a few torches and the catacombs light up in an eerie warm flickering glow. And same as we learned in school, the long hallways are lined with human bones, centuries of skeletons stacked upon each other in intricate patterns. I've never been one to spook easily, but this place gives me the absolute creeps.

Brisa and the other vamps know exactly where they're going, as if they've done this countless times. They probably have. "We have a safe place that the hunters don't know about," I hear one of the other vampires say to his fledgling. I swallow hard, for the first time praying that hunters don't show up. They wouldn't want to save me, not the way I am now. They'd count me as one of the vampires, a traitor to human kind. And I wouldn't blame them.

But they won't come, at least not mine. I already know they're weaker than ever.

There are eight fledglings by my count. Seven other humans who are choosing this life . . . or rather, this afterlife. One that will stretch on and on and on if they're lucky, filled with adventure and travel and darkness and blood and death and answering to somebody who has more control over their free will than maybe even they do. I don't understand how anyone could willingly sign up for this. It doesn't matter what I feel for Adrian, I still wouldn't want this. When I was younger, I read that book where the girl begs her vampire boyfriend to turn her, where turning eighteen felt like a horrible old age. I didn't understand it then, and I still don't now.

Why are people so afraid of death?

It's not like I have a death wish. I don't. But I want to live––*really* live.

I want to live a full life. That means having the sun. It means enjoying real food and drinks and going on vacations to discover places with blue skies overhead. I want to feel love and heartbreak and family––my own children––and time passing by as I grow old.

I never thought I wanted children, not in this horrible world, but maybe I would someday.

Not a family that is made from adults turning into immortal blood suckers, but real families with human problems and joys. The way that vampires create their families can't replace the real thing. I want to be a parent, I want my kids to have siblings and hopefully cousins and aunts and uncles and everything that goes with it. All the things I never got to have, those are the things I want my kids to have one day.

I've never really thought too much about a full human life, or maybe I've spent countless hours thinking about it.

But now it's all about to be taken away, and I can only desperately pray that Adrian's plan will work, that he was being honest, and that I can trust him. I can trust him, right? But then, why didn't he tell me that today would've been my last day? Why keep that a secret? He knew I had been waiting for this to happen and was growing impatient, so what isn't he telling me?

Maybe he just wanted to be with me. He could've waited until I gave into my attraction for him, but I don't think he'd be that selfish.

We reach an area with several small openings in the walls and stop. These are obviously the crypts we're to be placed in. They'll take our blood and give us theirs. They'll put us in that wall and allow the vampire venom to do its job, and in three days when they come back for us, we'll rise as one of them.

"This is where the transformation will happen." Brisa sounds like a proud parent. "We are taking care to separate you all because we can't have one vampire waking before the others. Let's just say you'll be very thirsty." The vampires chuckle at that, and my mouth goes sour.

Brisa turns to me. "And you, my darling, are the very first. Are you ready?"

No, of course I'm not ready, but I don't have a choice.

I smile down at her, she's so petite and beautiful, but worldly and powerful. I wish I could stake her and hate that I can't. She smiles back. "Please, my darling, keep your angel wings. I rather like them. I find it kind of ironic, don't you think? I mean, what better outfit than that of an angel for my very first princess."

I blink at her, reality snapping into place. "Your princess?"

"Oh, didn't Adrian tell you that? This agreement was made ages ago. Before you even came here, actually. The whole reason I wanted you to come was so I could vet you and see if you would be worthy of the title. So sorry we lied to you and said it would be him to do it. I wanted to make sure I liked you. Plus, I was waiting for him to take your virginity." She scrunches her nose. "I rather dislike the idea of a virginal vampire as my daughter, no offense."

My heart shatters and disbelief overtakes me. I stare between the two of them, and Adrian offers me nothing. Not an apology, not anger, not regret. *Nothing.* And suddenly, in the worst way, I know the answer to my recurrent question.

I cannot trust Adrian.

I never could.

And I am a fool to have believed him for even a second. I had weeks of chances to try to get out of this place and I didn't because he fed me some ridiculous plan about having someone get me out of here before the third day. What a load of crap that was. And I wanted to believe him, I chose to ignore the stupidity of his plan because the truth was that I wanted to be with him. I was falling in love with him, and he played that to his advantage. I'm nothing but a stupid little girl to him, someone to be used in whatever way he saw fit to please his queen and meet his own agendas. Maybe he never turned on me. Maybe he was never on my side to begin with.

And my virginity. Maybe that part hurts the most, because I gave him something Brisa wanted him to take. He never cared for me. It was all a lie. All of it.

"You've handed me over to your queen like a prize?" I ask him, a wobble in my voice betraying my attempt at stoicism.

"Brisa needs to build her line back up. You should be grateful she chose you," he responds, and then he melts into the crowd of vampires surrounding us. It doesn't make sense. I thought he hated her. Maybe he does, but he still did what was best for her over what was best for me--what he promised me.

"So, you'll be my master?" I ask Brisa, even though I already know the answer. I'm stalling. I'm in disbelief. I'm--

She answers by extending her fangs, grabbing hold of me, and sinking her teeth deep into my neck.

CHAPTER 30

My limbs go numb and then limp. Excruciating pain shoots through me, followed by exquisite euphoria. The bliss seemingly heals me, sending me away. One second I am standing, and the next I am on the ground, Brisa leaning over me, feeding on me like she's probably done to countless others before, but to me, it's like falling in love for the first time. I smile at her, enjoying every incredible second. I don't care that her venom stings because it's so wonderful, and much stronger than Hugo's was. Perhaps that's because she's the queen, and the oldest vampire alive.

The last of my thoughts run as dry as my veins.

She is lost to me, everything's in a fog, but my body is still incredibly alive. It's as if every cell is being rattled, shaken, burned, and transformed by her venom. Brisa sucks and sucks, drinking my blood until my vision blurs, the edges going black, and everything tunnels. I don't like that, so I close my eyes. I don't scream because I don't want her to stop. So I sigh, letting it happen, willing it to happen, whatever *it* is.

But somewhere, somehow, there is still a part of me that is fighting this, a part of me that's the little girl, that's the teenager, that's the grown woman. All of them are Eva, and she is lashing out. She wants her life back. And she wants Brisa dead.

I am that girl.

She is me.

But I am also this new thing, this soon-to-be vampire. Brisa finally pulls away but stays leaning over me, her amber eyes ablaze like hot coals. "I can taste Hugo's venom in you," she whispers low, eyes growing angrier by the second. She knew that he was going to take me as his own that night, but she didn't know that he had already fed. At least I don't think so, because with her, it's so hard to know what she's thinking. "I have half a mind to kill you right now," she sneers as her lips softly caress my cheek. "But once you are mine, Evangeline, you will be unable to resist anything I ask of you. You will be loyal to me through our bond. And perhaps that will be your punishment. Because if you hate me, this transformation will force you to love me instead." She inches back and smiles wickedly.

My mind slowly rolls back to me, and I search for Adrian, but he's not here. Where could he have possibly gone at a time like this? Does he really feel so little for me that he'd leave me here in my most vulnerable moment? But no, my most vulnerable moment already happened, and he was very much there for that. My heart crumbles all over again. Tears burn in my eyes as I search the faces of the people watching me. It's a sea of faces with predatory claims in their hungry eyes, as if they can smell the last of the human blood still left in my body. I look away and try to sit up, but it's useless. I've lost too much blood. I was strong once, and now I can hardly remember what that felt like.

Brisa holds her slim arm to my lips and blood fills my mouth. I start to choke on it and try to turn away but she's too strong and holds me in place. It flows down my throat and I gag on it for what feels like ages. When it's over, she lifts me easily into her cold arms as if I were nothing but a small child. Even though I've got at least twenty pounds on her, her vampire strength is unmatched. She walks me into the little crypt and lays me down on a flat slab bed.

"Sleep now, my little one," she coos like a madwoman, "for when you wake, your past will be nothing but a burdensome dream, and your true life will start." She steps away, watching me for a long moment with a satisfied smile. It's like she's tucking her child into bed, not killing a human. This is sadistic. This isn't what I want. The tears release from my eyes and stream down my cheeks, mixing with the wetness of my bloodied neck.

No. This can't happen.

She can't leave me here. Where's Adrian? Why can't I speak?

Will I be able to fight this on my own? Somehow, I know I won't.

A sob racks through me right as something burns, prickling at my hands. Is it the venom working its way through me? The fiery pain gets hotter and hotter, crawling its way up my arms.

Brisa steps back.

I finally find my voice. "What's happening to me?"

"I knew from the first moment that I saw you in person and had a chance to smell your blood that you were different," she says, "and I was thrilled. You had to be mine. Adrian agreed."

"Why?" My voice scratches at my throat. The burning continues.

She leans in and whispers against my ear. "Just between you and me, it's time for a new generation of royal children. Soon they'll all be replaced by worthier sons and daughters, even my precious Adrian must be culled. You think you hate me but, darling, that will change. Don't you see? You're exactly what I've been searching for."

Realization is like a sharp arrow to the chest. Brisa's the one who's been killing the princes––and pinning it on everyone else.

"But why me?" The question still remains.

"Because you're special. You're part of them, but now

you'll also be part of us. You're both--exactly what I need."

"I don't know what you're talking about." The pain intensifies, and I scream out, "Please stop this!"

A light flashes so bright that my eyes cannot handle it and I squeeze them shut. There's a scream--Brisa's scream--and then more screams that aren't hers. All the vampires, the fledglings, everyone . . .

And then there's nothing.

And I'm nothing.

CHAPTER 31

I don't know how long I'm lost to the heat. Hours? Days? Or maybe it's merely minutes. But I'm there for all of it, and I don't know what it means. Fear wracks me for the eternity that I lay waiting, terrified that I'm transforming into one of them. If I could crawl out of here I would, but I can't move. Finally, the burn dissipates enough for me to open my eyes and not be blinded by the light. I peer at my hands, but there's no sign of scorching. They're not even red.

I look around, expecting to be walled in here since that was the plan. Brick by horrid brick, we were to be locked into our crypts like a child in a mother's womb until it was time to be born again. But there's no wall keeping me in, and I stand, heading toward the entrance. When I peer out, I don't know what I'm expecting, but not this. Because it's nothing--nobody is here, no vampires to watch over us, no lights, no torches.

Just emptiness.

But I can see everything, every crack in the cobbled walls, every old bone stacked up, every booted footprint in the dirt, all of it. It's as if I've walked outside in the middle of the day rather than far under the city of love. Doesn't matter—I'm out of here.

I sprint my way down the stooped hallway of musty old bones and back up into the church and then outside, moving faster than I ever have before. The sun has already crested over the horizon and I immediately jump back into Notre Dame's shadows. Could this be it? Could this be my opportunity to end my life now instead of starting a new one as a monster? I always thought I would be able to offer myself to the sun if this happened, but now that I'm faced with the reality of my situation, I'm not so sure I'm strong enough.

I reach out a tentative hand, one finger pointed, prepared for it to burn into dust. I imagine the pain to be similar to what it was in the crypt, or maybe even worse, but when it slides into the sunlight, nothing happens. The light wraps around my fingertips, same as it always has. I slowly step the rest of the way out, and still nothing happens. I sigh in relief, sobs once again wracking my body. I fall to my knees and tuck my head against my chest, crying. I've never been much of a crier, but this moment is perhaps the one I'm most grateful for in my entire life. Because I'm alive. I'm here. I'm safe. And I'm still me.

And at this point, all I can do is cling to the hope that

Adrian didn't lie to me about this one important thing. He claimed that if I didn't stay for the three nights that I could avoid this transformation. I growl to myself because how can I trust anything he's ever said? And how could I have been so stupid as to let him manipulate me like he did? I walked into his trap willingly! He's proved who his loyalty is to, and it isn't to me.

I sigh and stand back up, walking out to the sidewalk. My transformation hasn't happened, and I'm worried that maybe I have too much venom, maybe it will kill me, but maybe it's exactly what I need to set me free. My senses are full-on. With Hugo, they'd come and go, but now that I have Brisa's venom in my veins, I am ablaze with power.

And it's time to run.

There isn't a snowball's chance in hell that I'm going back into that crypt or anywhere near a graveyard ever again, nor am I going around vampires anytime soon. I'm about to become a hunted woman, is my guess. Thank goodness it's daylight because I have to get out of here. I need to find a way to escape Paris and never return. Where should I go? Where can I be safe from them? They can smell me, that I already know, but will they be able to smell me enough that I can't take on another identity? Because if they find me, I'm as good as dead. I can fight and I'll take down as many as I can, but I know what Brisa is capable of, and I know her numbers.

My mind whirls with possibilities and then it hits me; I can't go back to New Orleans. Ever.

The realization hurts perhaps more than anything else. Maybe even more than realizing Adrian betrayed me, had kept important secrets from me. He knew I would resist the moment when his queen took me, and so he never said a word. He knew, and there's nothing he could ever do or say to make me forgive him. I'm done trusting vampires, and I'm done with him.

My hands continue to burn, but no light escapes from them. I think back to what I saw with that blinding light, not wanting to admit it, but forcing myself to anyway. My palms had light exploding from them, the brightest light I've ever seen. I fist my hands at the thought, wishing they were cool. Maybe I'll find a place where I can dip them in the river. The sidewalk I'm on is wide and stretches for miles. The river is below, but unreachable from here. I keep walking. Take this one step at a time. First, wet my hands and cool the burn. Second, get out of here and find somewhere safe to hide. And finally, figure out what is happening to me.

A little red convertible sports car with the hood back pulls up next to me, screeching to a halt. The face that peers up at me from the driver's seat makes me stop in surprise. I don't know who I expected to find me. Felix, maybe? But I saw the look on his face, he'll never forgive me for what I did with Adrian. In my weeks at Versailles, I kept imagining my friends busting me out of the palace. What an idiot I was to give up on them. When they needed me most, I was useless. And Kenton paid the ultimate price.

No, it's not them smiling at me, and it never will be again.

It's Leslie Tate. "Climb inside, Eva," he says wearily, "we have so much to discuss."

I step back, about ready to jump into that river to get away from him. The last thing I need is another man intent on using me for his own agenda. "Did you send them in there? Was that your doing?"

"They would've with or without my help," he insists.

"How would they even know where to look? You came into Adrian's suite that night of the attack. What did you take?"

"Join me and I'll tell you."

I glare.

He puffs out his breath. "Listen, Brisa's takeover of Versailles is international news. Once your friends figured out that's where you'd most likely be, they came to me. Not the other way around."

"I'm done with you," I growl out, and then I start walking again. He drives beside me and I keep talking. "Look, I know you're something different, okay? I know you were willing to slaughter my friends to get at Adrian. And that tells me all I need to know about someone like you."

"Get in the car, or I will make you get in the car," he calls back, "this isn't a negotiation."

"I can't trust you." I laugh maniacally. "You can go now."

"Believe me, Eva, you can't trust anyone. But that's not what's important right now. Right now, we have to get you to safety, and I know how to do that."

"I can take care of myself." Other vehicles go around him and some of them honk. It's early enough that he doesn't slow traffic down too much, but try telling that to the taxi cabs. Not that he's the type to care.

"Don't you wanna know what you are?" he calls out. "Do you want to know what's happening to you?"

I don't look at him even though my interest piques. I open and close my hands, but I already know the light has vanished. My hands are normal, and maybe it's a good thing that he didn't see what I saw in that crypt.

Or maybe it's all in my head. Maybe it was some kind of hallucination from Brisa's strong venom. But no . . . that couldn't be. Because I wasn't sealed into that crypt. Because Brisa responded with words about who I was. Because when that prickling happened in my hands, the flash of light followed. And then the screams. And then nothing.

I stop short with a gasp.

Is it possible? Did I kill the vampires? What kind of light did I emit down there?

And if she's dead, then the vampires of the world are now subject to whoever their highest masters are in the bloodlines, masters who might want to hurt the humans far more than she ever did. And if word gets out about what I did, then I'll become the most wanted person on planet Earth.

For once, I hope a vampire is alive and well . . .

I stop and walk over to Tate, leaning over the edge of the car. "Can you really help me?"

"I can really help you." He nods. "Now please, Eva, get inside because we don't have much time."

I have nowhere else to go.

No one else is willing to help me but him.

And most of all, I need answers.

So against my better judgement, I do what he says, opening the car door and sliding into the passenger's seat. He speeds away before I even have a chance to buckle myself in. The air whips through my hair; it's mostly down by now. And my makeup must be a mess. And my dress is torn and bloody. I'm still wearing the sheer angel wings. I reach back and untangle them from my dress, then toss them out. Let someone else have them or let them be garbage, but I don't *ever* want to see them again.

As we drive out of the city, we sit in silence, nothing but the wind to listen to. We drive and drive and drive, a race against the sun. And somehow, deep down, I know that he's taking me somewhere I've been waiting to go my whole life--because whatever Tate is must be what-ever I am, too. I didn't want to face it, but it explains why I was never able to see my own aura, why the vampires took such an interest in me, why Remi gave me that wink, why Brisa said what she said before the light took over.

Her last words echo in my mind: *Because you're special. Because you're both.*

Adrian

A LETTER FROM NINA

Make sure to get ready for Wicked Sun! And thank you for reading Cruel Stakes--I hope you enjoyed this story. I wrote it during one of the hardest times of my life, and found a lot of escapism in this world and with these characters. Thank you to the fans of the series for keeping this alive and the momentum going. I love you so much for what you did for me. If you haven't read the Blood Vow bonus scene yet, please join Nina's Reading Party on Facebook and get that.

Happy Reading,

Nina

ACKNOWLEDGMENTS

Thank you to my editor Ailene Kubricky, cover designer Yocla Book Designs, proof readers Sarah Mostaghel, Kate Anderson, and Cassie Buethe, the ARC team, and all the readers for making this happen. Thank you to my husband Travis and my mom Karren for all you did for me during a really tough time. I'm beyond grateful for everyone's love and support.

ABOUT THE AUTHOR

Nina Walker writes YA paranormal romance, urban fantasy, dystopian fantasy and more. *Cruel Stakes* is her 14th novel. She lives in Southern Utah with her sweetheart, 2 kids, and 3 pets. She loves to spend as much time outdoors exploring the real world as she does exploring other authors' brilliant imaginations.

www.ninawalkerbooks.com

Facebook Reader Group "Nina's Reading Party"

Instagram @NinaBelievesInMagic

TikTok is @ninawalker.books.

CPSIA information can be obtained
at www.ICGtesting.com
Printed in the USA
LVHW031926201021
700970LV00005B/842

9 781950 093274